THE COMPROMISE

Adam Loretz

PROLOGUE

Rewind to 1995. People-smuggling, pedophile rings and investigations into morally corrupt celebrities are glamorised in everyday headlines and become the lyrics to which youth culture sing to, dance to and believe in. From this new desensitised normality, the grotesque, morally corrupt goings-on, make normal life seem like a living nightmare, where anything can and will happen.

We're safe in the UK, for several decades, our war has been viewed on foreign soil, through a TV screen; in Northern Ireland, the Gulf and now Bosnia. Back home another war prevails in the subterfuge of the music. Youth culture is zoned out to phat basslines; the thrills, bellyaches and oblivion of raving, to the posturing of hip-hop gangsters; gun toting, blunt smoking badasses, turning the 9mm sideways, firing out debauched hood shit as genius, catchy raps. The kids party hard, living for the weekend high, a high supplied by an international, underworld network.

Between these facts and a real-life journey

to Liverpool for a young student named Aitch, the following could easily be true. Sorry, Aitch, there's no waking up from this bad dream.

CHAPTER ONE

STOCKHOLM
Last Week

Alvar's watch read 12.37 p.m., it was time to do this. He zipped up his padded jacket, touched his shoulder rig and the carefully rolled-up ski mask on his head and slipped out of his pickup truck. He carefully opened the tailgate and climbed up on the flatbed. He tapped the tarp, which was still strapped over the case, and crouched, motionless, to take in the view down the street. Through the thick glass of his circular spectacles his tiny eyes analysed the building. At a glance, the stocky guy was almost invisible in his dark clothes, only his breath gave him away in the cold, night air.

From this vantage point he could probably hit the door, which would take down the back wall of the biker bar. His mind was made up and, still breathing out of the side of his mouth, he drew his eyes back from the building to the row of rain-soaked motorcycles glistening in front of the Damascus MC clubhouse. The last two weeks, things had heated up between the two motorcycle gangs that ran the city, and as far as Alvar was concerned, this wasn't revenge or just retaliation, the Damascus crew had something bigger coming: annihilation. Alvar checked his watch, Kenny would be here in a minute, so he untied the tarp straps. *Showtime*, Alvar thought and blew gently through his cupped hands, his knuckles reading BADBONES MC. Alvar held still, eyes locked on the industrial-looking building, listening to his prey; the sounds of clinking glasses, pool balls cracking and the deep bass of death metal music vibrating a soul-swamping danger in the darkness.

Inside, the packed biker bar buzzed like a demonic pinball machine. Stockholm's dominant chapter: all ex-conscripts, laughing and drinking, at ease in their military and motorcycle boots, leathers, ripped denims and greasy hair.

Three Damascus guys lined up shots, downed them swiftly, then turned to take in the commotion. Cain looked at his empty shot glass, then to his two sergeants-at-arms, "I gotta get back to the hospital," Cain said, wiping his moustache and patting his heart. "You good to step up, Anders?"

"Not even a question, brother. Enjoy fatherhood, again!" Anders said, as the two clasped hands firmly. Cain grabbed his keys to leave, Anders resumed his game, the pool cue sliding back over his thumb and punching straight back, exploding into the triangle of colourful balls.

Outside, Kenny lifted a huge green box on the back of the pickup and slid it to Alvar, who opened the security latches with a satisfying clunk. Alvar grinned and laughed with nervous excitement, "Is this what I read about, Kenny?"

The craggy-faced South African smiled wryly, keeping an eye on Alvar as he lifted the lid to inspect the contents. "One in, one out," Alvar said, as he pushed an old, brown leather suitcase with his jackboot back to Kenny. The old guy flipped the brass suitcase catches. He noted the eight Glock 19s; the small, distinctive pistols, randomly chucked in next to a clear, plastic box which contained six neat stacks of banknotes.

"What am I doing with these Glocks?" Kenny asked.

"They're all tainted. Stick them in the crusher," Alvar replied.

"Alright man," Kenny said closing the suitcase and reaching into his reversible blue Puffa to grab a cigarette from the camouflaged interior. Alvar looked back down the street again at the biker bar. Like all Swedes, he'd done national service and knew the drill. Alvar pushed his glasses up his rain-soaked face, cursing the weather, and ran his other hand over the box of projectiles. Kenny breathed out smoke as he cautioned, "Load only when you intend to fire, my friend."

Alvar turned back resolutely, holding the

rocket launcher casually. "This isn't about turf anymore. This is war."

He picked up a projectile, inserted it, took aim at the door of his enemy and squeezed the trigger, all without hesitation. The rocket launcher gave a short kick followed by a soft blast of smoke. The missile tore through the air and exploded in a deafening blast, hurling fiery rubble and toppling the row of motorcycles. An instant grey transition revealed the demolished clubhouse as an angry, squint-inducing wave of dust rippled towards Alvar and Kenny.

GERMANY

Blair sat dishevelled and alone in the cab of the Mercedes sprinter van. He ruminated over his bandaged left hand that was resting on the steering wheel. He smoothed down his goatee which was almost lost in five days' beard growth, his teeth scraping over his dry lips. The birthday napkin full of cake was still on the dashboard. Some party *that* was! His eyes fell back to the ancient photo he held in his right hand of the pretty twenty-year-old girl, his ex, Nina. It had been well over a decade, but recently she had come back to haunt him. He looked at the picture. The picture seemed to look back at him. "Fuck it!" he reeled, and hit the dash board three times.

His hackles were up. He took a good, long breath. He'd stared at Nina's picture for a few days now, wondering if kicking her into touch all those years ago had been the right choice. "Yeah, course it was," he instinctively told himself, trying to stay calm, smoothing back his long hair and tying it into a ponytail. Blair had never looked back, never had to, until now.

He looked out through the dirty windscreen at the dissolving horizon. This was an easy job, but since the kids' party Blair's mind had been unravelling a lot of family shit. Sandie had a way of doing that to him, cos of the promise he'd made to her, at her sister Jackie's funeral. A promise that he hadn't kept.

At the time, Blair had been a committed soldier, fighting in Ireland, Bosnia and Iraq. However, after Jackie's fatal accident and his older brother Frank getting banged up again for a four-year stretch, someone had had to step in and look after their kid, Little Al. Sandie suddenly became a mum, a good one, and Blair had quit the army and more than filled Frank's shoes. It was still dangerous work, but it paid royally. Tonight's deal, the biggest and dodgiest yet, was in completely foreign territory. Blair could feel the pressure of it all; all of these expectations closing in on him and it made him fucking uncomfortable – even if it paid for all his shit, it wasn't worth it.

Pat, pat, pat and the rain started to blur out the world. Blair sat back and closed his eyes and that was wrong too, instantly remembering how Little Al had hugged him so tight, that he'd had to double-tap his submission. Blair opened his eyes and let out a slow breath; he nodded in affirmation, the all-consuming self-loathing, swearing obscenities, flashing red in his mind.

Kenny knocked on the side of the van, giving Blair a start. Jumping out of the cab, Blair landed in a puddle and sloshed around to the flat tyre in his now-soaked, white Adidas trainers. Kenny retired to the cab on the opposite side of the white van, yin to Blair's emerging yang. Blair could feel the energy rising; he took one look at the flat rear tyre, opened his green parka and gave it a swift kick. He looked down at his white shell toes, now ruined with a dirty black mark across them.

"Shite!" he muttered in his Liverpudlian accent. Tapping the driver's window, Blair called out for the jack. As Kenny opened the floor panel, Blair shed his parka and bulletproof vest, tucking Nina's picture into his wallet for safekeeping. Taking the jack in his bandaged left hand, he struggled on his knees to lever up the Mercedes.

On the other side of the exhaust system, unseen by Blair, a small blinking tracker flashed *red, red, red*.

Kenny sauntered over and parked himself casually on the side of the van. He felt in the pocket of his reversible Puffa, wearing it camouflage side out today, useless against the white van. He pulled out and flicked open his Zippo. The broken lines of the old South Africans face lit up in a flash as he ignited the flame and sucked the life out of a cigarette, exhaling the fumes slowly through his nose. "Easiest money you'll ever make!" He said, raising his eyebrows.

Blair wrestled clumsily with the wheel nuts, as cold spots of rain turned quickly into a heavy downpour, the bandage unravelling to reveal the ugly burn on his left hand. "This ain't a party trick, Kenny!" He pulled his sleeves up, revealing his old battalion ink, a Staffordshire bull terrier on his forearm. *Fuck this!* Blair thought, as the rain ran into his eyes. He had to see this through, even if his instincts were screaming for him to bolt.

Kenny narrowed his eyes, taking another drag, his hand protecting the cigarette from the downpour.

The ex-soldier finally freed the flat tyre, and as he stood up Kenny stuck the ciggy in his mouth, stepped up and grabbed Blair's collar.

"You seem distracted, what's got under your skin?" the South African demanded, the heat and smoke of his cigarette torturing Blair.

"Nothing you need to worry about," Blair replied, leaning back from the stench and smoke.

Kenny tugged Blair's collar again, their faces an inch apart. Kenny took another drag and removed the cigarette from his mouth. "Mal recommended you highly. I don't need you losing your focus, right?" Kenny said, exhaling smoke at

Blair.

Blair leaned in stoically and pointed to his eyes with the fingers of his bandaged hand: "I got lasers, mate. Don't worry, nothing wrong with my trigger finger."

Kenny took a second and let go of Blair.

Blair looked down, tapped his feet in the puddle and laughed.

"Shii-it! Sixteen years' service, you'd think I'd have worn my old boots for this gig!"

Kenny looked down at Blair's soaking trainers and returned to the cab shaking his head, flicking away the end of his lit cigarette.

Lifting the flat tyre into the back of the van, Blair swore as the wheel pulled the edge of a tarp, sliding it off the cargo and revealing an open crate of AK-47s. Time to focus. He couldn't change the past but the future was his to choose. Kenny banged the side of the van, shouting to hurry up – they were already behind schedule.

LIVERPOOL
Last week

Dusk settled over the terrace as Sandie stood guard at her doorstep, buttoned up in her dungarees against the chill and her outlaw in-law Blair. Inside, the front window was crammed; a homemade banner read HAPPY BIRTHDAY LITTLE AL, 4 TODAY. The kid and his young guests bounced in the front window to Wu-Tang's, 'Protect Ya Neck' in fancy dress – a mix of mostly black and white striped burglar tops, armed police fatigues and orange jail jumpsuits.

"I thought you were having a wild west party?" Blair asked Sandie.

"The costume shop ran out of ten-gallon hats, so now we're havin' a cops 'n' robbers bash," Sandie explained. "Why do you'se lot want to come to a kids' party for anyway? Paul'll go off his head if he knew you were here."

"Is he here?" Blair asked.

"No, he's doing a late shift," Sandie replied.

Blair shrugged, "Look Sandie, my brother can't miss another one of Little Al's birthdays."

Sandie's face grew serious as she peered around Blair to glare at the black BMW across the street. "But … Frank's not out the nick until next Tuesday?"

Blair took Sandie's hand and motioned over his shoulder, pointing to the Beemer. "I know, that's why Me, Mal and Sparkie are here. Show face for our kid and, our Sparkie's got a video camera and all. Just let him film Little Al blowin' out the candles and we'll be out of your hair. Promise."

Sandie screwed up her lips, visibly shaken as she fumed, "Our kid? I'm the one that's been holding the baby since my sister died. You got no idea of what I've sacrificed to raise that boy."

"Uncle Blair!" Little Al screamed, the kid standing in a heavy coat, shirt, tie and fedora behind the large front window.

Oblivious to her outrage, Blair stood looking back at Little Al, smirking to himself at the kid's costume. He turned to Sandie, "He's Al Capone, right? Brilliant!" he said, the real-life gangsters reflection masking that of the child mob boss.

Sandie remained stone-faced as Blair claimed, "I'd do anything for our brother's kid."

Incredulous, Sandie challenged him: "Really? You know, I hoped you'd have kept your promise when you left the army. The boy needs a father figure, but no, you've never stepped up, have ya?"

"Don't get mad at me, Sandie," Blair deflected. "Going to war, you know, changed me, gave me ... fucking, demons. I gotta live with that shit, day and night."

He gestured to Little Al just feet away. "Look, all I know is Mal wants to give the kid a present. Just look at his face. How can you say no to that?"

Sandie fumed at the audacity on display: "Bloody Mal. He may be the kid's bloody godfather, he could be bloody Marlon Brando his flamin' self, I don't want him or any of you lot swaggering in here, with your fancy camera and expensive gifts, acting like you give a toss, so just ... go, will ya!"

As Sandie moved to slam the door, Blair

wedged his foot in. "Wait, wait, wait," he pleaded, taking a slow breath.

"I'm gonna make sure it's a fresh start for Frank. Okay? No more drinking, nothing. On the level. No more getting banged up."

Sandie glimpsed the fifty-pound note Blair had slipped into her hand and recoiled. "Don't make empty promises or palm me off with your dirty money. *I* paid for this party."

She gave Blair a shove and he stumbled in a circle as she shouted, "Now clear off!"

Blair took another deep breath, coming back slower. "Look, we both know Frank can be a total knobhead … at times, but he's still my brother … and I'm … Little Al's favourite uncle."

"You're his only uncle, you twerp!" Sandie shot back.

"Exactly. Numero uno," Blair persisted, tapping his finger to his chest, just as the house lights cut out.

Little Al appeared, wiping his steamed-up glasses. "Auntie Sandie, we need a pound for the meter!"

Sandie sighed in resignation. "Got change for a fifty?"

Seeing Blair's satisfied smile, she exhaled with a conciliatory nod for him to enter. At that, Blair turned and whistled at the waiting BMW, out of which came two men. Little Al's godfather

Mal carried a huge, gift-wrapped box, the ex-bodybuilder still posing, shoulders back, exuding confidence. From the driver's side followed a scrawny younger man, Sparkie, his body lost in a shell-suit, pointing a small video camera at Mal, it's red light on, already recording.

GERMANY
Present

The ageing engine of the Mercedes van seemed to growl as it rumbled down the dark, pine-lined road. Blair gripped the steering wheel, finishing off the slice of birthday cake as he drove. His eyes occasionally flicked to the fading photo of Nina tucked into the corner of the dashboard.

In the passenger seat, Kenny squirmed, an open newspaper crinkling in his hands.

"Did you shave your nuts last night, or what?" Blair suddenly asked, breaking the silence.

Kenny raised an eyebrow, attention still on the Swedish newspaper headline about last week's rocket attack in Stockholm.

Kenny tapped the photo of the nightclub in ruins. "Says here the Damascus MC and Badbones are now at war. Yes!"

He smacked the paper with the back of his hand, but Blair kept his eyes fixed ahead on the dark road, letting off steam, his hackles getting the better of him.

"Stop right there, Kenny." Blair glanced at the arms dealer. "Bosnia was a war. The Falklands was a war," he said bluntly. "The Badbones mob are just trying to scare the Damascus crew. Trust me. It ain't a fucking war until bullets are pinging past your ears in a sustained attack."

Kenny jabbed his finger at the image of destruction. "This … this is just the beginning. The shipment we've got here for the Damascus crew will escalate everything. And … a regular job for us, if you want it," Kenny said, looking over the top of the newspaper at Blair.

The van's oil light suddenly flashed. Blair's jaw tightened. "Maybe."

"What's there to think about?" Kenny asked.

Blair's knuckles whitened on the wheel. "Everything. Because we're fuelling the fire and I don't like getting burned."

Kenny waved a dismissive hand. "Don't be so dramatic. I told you, this Cain guy just needs a quick weapons demo from us and we're out of there. Easy money. I've got the targets," he said, opening a map book to reveal some printed shooting targets.

"I hope the bastard can shoot straight!" Blair said letting out his breathe.

Kenny pointed his finger into Blair's right eye line: "This is the crossroads."

Blair didn't flinch, just reacted with a hard

left turn, sending Kenny flying across the seats into the passenger window. The van careered down the narrow, bumpy dirt track, Kenny's arms flailing to grab the hand strap above his head as pine branches scraped eerily across the metal side of the sprinter van as they plunged deeper into the dark forest.

*

Whilst the old Volvo 240 estate was his wife's car, it was still surprisingly peppy and the right choice for the tail. The innocuous maroon vehicle charged along, and Per had to be mindful he didn't get too close to the sprinter van. He eased off the accelerator and turned to his passenger, Alvar, "This is it. Check the pistol in the glove box."

Alvar nodded, his round glasses now featuring pink surgical tape on the nose piece. "I'll put this away, then," he said, placing the tracking receiver in the glove box next to a ball of red wool. Behind the wool he picked out a Tec-9, a pistol-sized machine-gun, and inserted a clip. "There's a parallel road just up ahead," Alvar continued, racking the bolt and pushing in the safety.

LIVERPOOL
Last week

It was chaos in Sandie's modest terrace house. The rambunctious, half-pint-sized revellers tore about the tiny kitchen that opened into the now-crowded front room, filled with torn wrapping paper, disposable plates laden with half-eaten cheese sandwiches and plastic cups of cola. The radio played 'Gangsta's Paradise' as the smell of buttercream and vanilla birthday cake wafted through the air.

Sandie tried to ignore seven-year-old Caspar, dressed as a police firearms officer. She gave him thirty seconds. He lurked about the wallpaper table, covered in plates and bowls of party food, hands behind his back, inspecting the offerings. She turned for a moment to get the birthday cake candles, then back, catching him red-handed. "Caspar, get your fingers out of the potato salad!" Sandie scolded. Caspar quickly sucked the creamy potatoes off of his fingers and scampered away, grinning impishly. He'd only made it seventeen seconds.

In the front room, Mal and Little Al were unwrapping his gift, a large Scalextric racetrack set, as the hyperactive kids carried on noisily obliterating each other with their toy guns. The heat and excitement was getting to Mal, the big man slipping off his weighted leather blazer, a pair of lightweight fleecy gloves disguising the heavy contents of his open pockets.

Sandie emerged from the kitchen carrying the birthday cake, the candles flickering as she started everyone singing 'Happy Birthday' to Little

Al.

As everyone sang, Blair looked to Sandie, then to Mal and then into the black lens of the video camera, as unnerving as a shark's eye. Blair parried the lens and looked out the window until the song finished.

"Hey, Al, have you got a message for your daddy?" Mal asked.

Little Al replied wistfully, "I wish you and Mummy were here."

Mal stood up, taking a big gulp, beads of sweat now trickling down his face. He dabbed at his eyes with a party napkin. Once he was done, he looked to Sparkie who nodded approvingly, the camera still rolling on the party mayhem.

In the kitchen, the kettle began to boil as Little Al ran in brandishing a toy machine-gun. Blair gently redirected the barrel away from him and got down to wipe some icing off Little Al's chin. "Nice beard, Capone! Jeez, you're sweating like you stole this!"

"I'm a scouser, ain't I!" Little Al replied.

Blair gently pinched his cheek, took his empty plastic cup and refilled it with Coke. The kid chugged it and threw himself at Blair, hugging him tighter and tighter. "Love you, Uncle Blair," the kid said into the gangster's ear. Blair blinked, off guard, tried to swallow, but couldn't. Blair double-tapped the lad's arm. The kid sprang up and raced back to his friends, filling them with a full magazine of imaginary bullets. Blair stood and filled his lungs trying to look unfazed.

Sandie watched pensively as Blair picked up a framed photo of her late sister Jackie with Little Al. "I've never seen this one of your sister before – Jackie looks dead happy here," Blair remarked. "Oh, fuck's sake, I'm sorry, slipped out!"

Sandie brushed it off, "Forget about it, Doctor Freud. That was the last picture ever taken of my sister and Little Al – *you* were in Bosnia."

Blair turned the frame to face the party. He picked up some holiday brochures on the kitchen side, "Going somewhere nice?"

"If we can afford it. Got to make memories for Little Al, right?" Sandie replied.

"Frank'll be getting out of prison soon," Blair retorted raising his eyebrows.

Sandie shook her head, she knew the score. "Don't give me that. You and I know the truth. He'll be rubbing shoulders with Mal soon as he's out. No, Frank won't be taking the boy on *any* holidays."

Blair couldn't follow that, or return her gaze. He looked down and thumbed through a cookbook that lay underneath the brochures. He stopped at a bookmarked page, looking closer at it, registering it was a photo of himself, dressed in desert-storm fatigues, his arm around an old ex-girlfriend, Nina.

"What's this old relic doing in here?"

"Pride of the family, you were, soldier boy. You had everything, you and Nina. If only you'd stayed together," Sandie remarked.

Scoffing, Blair retorted: "I was twenty-two, who knows anything about love and life at twenty-two!"

Sandie insisted "Well, what I know is that girl worshipped you!"

Blair looked up, surprised.

"Really," Sandie went on, "she could have been the one!"

Blair looked unsettled. "Nah! I don't need a ball and chain, or three stripes on me arm to be happy."

"Well, you missed the boat on life's journey with Nina."

"I didn't miss any fucking boat. I dumped her!" He scolded quietly, stepping in to her.

Sandie recoiled, trailing her hand down him, "Hmm ... and look at you now, what have you got? Really?"

Blair pulled out a huge wad of cash, the bills bristling under his thumb. "This is what I've got, and this sound never gets old!"

Sandie frowned disapprovingly. "All the money in the world won't make you a good man," she said, then turned to get the coffee mugs. Her back turned, Blair slipped some fifties into her cookbook and shut it quietly.

"Where's Nina now, eh?" Blair enquired to Sandie's back.

Sandie turned to him, dizzying her head as she smiled sardonically.

"She married a really nice guy, actually – Neil – into property and that. Lives in Saudi. Got three kids."

Blair sucked his teeth derisively, stood tall, then swaggered off to watch Mal racing Little Al on the Scalextric track. Little Al was elated. Blair spied the birthday cake and wrapped up a good wedge in a colourful party napkin and slipped it into his jacket pocket.

Caspar came running down the stairs shouting, "Which one of you'se nicked my gun?"

Mal looked up and his Scalextric car flew off the electrified track as Caspar stormed past Blair. He looked at all the other boys' guns, investigating the torn-up wrapping paper, feeling between the settee cushions. Blair stood by the fireplace, for once allowing himself to get lost in the past, at the old photos of his roguish, extended family.

"Coffee's ready!" Sandie called, walking in from the kitchen. Blair turned to Sandie as Caspar began making shooting noises, swinging his arms around, capping everybody. Caspar jumped in front of Blair pointing Mal's Beretta pistol directly at him. "Bang! You're dead!" the boy yelled.

Blair instinctively grabbed the kid's wrist, pointing the gun straight up as it went off, shooting a hole in the ceiling. Plaster dropped on Sandie's head and she shrieked, dropping the tray of steaming coffees, her hands reaching up to her hair. The hot coffees toppled off of the tray, scalding Blair's left hand. He felt a shot of pain up his arm and drew it back quickly, smacking Sparkie, who in turn dropped the coffee-soaked video camera onto the stone fireplace with a crack. The terrified children scattered in all directions, the crisp noise of a real gunshot sending them into a real panic.

Blair carefully grabbed Caspar's wrist and pried away the pistol. Situation neutralised he turned and plunged his burned left hand into a jug of orange squash. Little Al ran crying into Auntie Sandie's arms, holding her tightly.

Sandie pointed accusingly at Sparkie, Mal and Blair, "You lot cannot be a part of Little Al's life *anymore*! You can't protect him and you don't love him. *This* isn't love! Don't turn up on match day, don't call and we *don't* want your dirty money. Now get out of my house!"

She smashed the fifty-pound note back into Blair's left hand and yanked away the jug of squash, before grabbing the wet video camera and hurling it at Sparkie. The party was well and truly over.

CHAPTER TWO

GERMANY
Present

The Mercedes van pulled up before the sloped track met the flat squared-off fire break area between the dense pine forest. It gave Blair a chance to look down on the secluded area, which was barely sixty metres square, in the middle of which was a blue van, disappearing in the fading light. Blair felt about in his parka pockets and fished out a headtorch, which he put on. The blue van flashed its headlights three times in greeting. Blair opened the window and winced, letting his injured, wet hand hang outside as he and Kenny continued down the slope to the meet. The cold air numbed his hand which bounced gently on the driver's door and calmed his warm, wet eyes.

Watching through binoculars and a sniper scope from their camouflaged position, Per and Alvar observed the Mercedes parking back-to-back with the blue van. Alvar watched through the scope, carefully holding the forestock which had 'BadBones' engraved on it. His earpiece crackled with a test call from Per. Alvar pressed his comms button and nodded to Per who nodded back. Alvar collected up his shooting sticks and moved off to find a position, his Tec-9 hanging on his back. Per checked his bag, containing three grenades and two smoke bombs, then pulled up his holstered .44 Magnum and double-checked the chambers of the cylinder were loaded. He was ready.

Meanwhile, Kenny walked to the clearing's edge and set up a target. Alvar froze as he spotted Kenny in his scope. *The double-dealing bastard!* he thought.

Cain stood with two of his soldiers by the blue van. At his signal, they stepped back. Blair handed Cain a short-stock AK-47 with a scope.

"No, no, no. You don't have an Uzi? Uzi is smaller."

"Trust me, you don't want an Uzi," Blair insisted, "This is a short stock AK-47 – the world's favorite killing machine, bonza!"

Cain looked unimpressed, Blair got serious.

"Look, mate, you want to spray and pray, or shoot the fucking eyebrows off a housefly at three hundred metres?"

The two stared each other out until Blair whistled to Kenny, who gave two whistles back. At Blair's hand signal, Kenny stood by the target. "Pick three numbers between one and ten," Blair told Cain.

"Two, five and ten."

With perfect precision, Blair executed each number. Kenny replaced the punctured target with a fresh one.

Watching through his scope, Alvar started to set up his shooting stick but stopped when Cain fired at the new target. Kenny ran up to show Cain the results. Cain leaned into Kenny holding the sieve-like target, clearly impressed.

"Now, we were told there would be pistols," Cain stated.

"Eric will be along shortly with a selection and … the other merchandise," Kenny replied.

Blair looked quizzically at Kenny.

Through his scope, Alvar took aim. "I'm in position, over."

"Get ready for my command, over," Per replied.

In the clearing a Ford transit van pulled up. Through Alvar's scope it blocked out his targets.

Per picked up a smoke grenade. "Take the shot, over." Per continued.

"Target obscured! Over."

Eric hopped out of the transit and shook Cain's hand.

Kenny interrupted, "Blair will just need to

check over the pistols. They were only collected earlier today."

Blair looked at Eric, then to Kenny, who narrowed his eyes and nodded stiffly for Blair to get the job done.

The back of Eric's van was pitch black. Blair could just about see an old, dusty leather case, and pulled it towards him and switched on his headtorch to examine the contents. Inside, the eight Glock 19 pistols shone under the direct beam of light. Blair shook his head with concern, inspecting one of the weapons, 'Badbones' engraved on the black handle.

Watching through his scope, Alvar pressed his comms button and spoke quietly, "Holy shit, Per, I was right, check the guy at the transit. Kenny is trying to sell our old fucking guns. Should I take this guy out? Over."

"Hold fire. How do you know they are ours? Over." Per asked.

"It's the Glock 19s, man, and they're still in that piece of shit leather suitcase, over."

"No, this guy is not a principal target. Wait for a tighter group with the buyer and my command, over," Per replied.

"Copy that, over," replied the spectacled sniper.

Something was about to happen, Blair could feel it. He stood still and listened closely for a second and then a metal noise reverberated from the back of the dark transit. Blair turned, and in the bright light of his headtorch the desperate eyes of a young, redheaded woman connected with him. She sat, her mouth was taped, arms and feet bound. Blair put his finger to his lips.

"Eric!" Blair called angrily.

Per readied a smoke grenade, rolling it around in his hand, ready. Through Alvar's scope Blair faced off with Eric. Eric pushed Blair who turned off his head torch and came back to his superior.

"I gave my word this Badbones shipment would be thrown in a crusher," Blair said.

"New plan. You got two minutes to make them ready to sell," Eric snarled.

"Nah. Not happening."

Eric stood in, toe-to-toe with Blair. "No?" his snarl opening to reveal his gappy,

clenched teeth.

Alvar moved the crosshairs from Blair to Cain.

"No," Blair said in calm defiance.

Eric turned his cheek and snapped back, slicing up through Blair's goose-down coat from bottom to top with a small razor blade. Blair caught the blade hand, now by his chest, Eric parrying, pushing a Glock pistol across the tangle of arms into Blair's cheek.

Alvar's finger twitched next to the trigger.

As the white goose feathers floated down around them, Blair slowly released Eric's hand, the Glock still pointing between his eyes. "Next time you tell me no, you'll spill more than feathers. Just take the girl to their truck and *you*, you and I, are done."

Alvar followed Eric as he grabbed the leather suitcase and carried it over to the Damascus crew's truck, next to Kenny and Cain.

In the van, Blair switched his headtorch back on. The girl's eyes widened in terror. Grinding his teeth, Blair made eye contact, "Don't worry, I'm gonna get you out of this, I promise." She nodded anxiously and Blair knew what to do.

"I have the targets in my sights, over," Alvar reported.

"Wait until the buyer is with the group, then wait for my command, over," Per said, as he pulled the pin on the smoke grenade.

Adrenaline exploded throughout Blair as he jumped out the back of the transit and hopped into the driver's seat of Eric's van.

"Target obtained, over," Alvar affirmed.

"Execute," Per instructed, as he turned and lobbed the smoke grenade from his sweating hand towards the parked trucks. A cloud instantly mushroomed; Eric turned, revealing Kenny.

Not too much gas! Blair thought, the wheels throwing up dirt, the Transit a millisecond from escaping this nightmare.

Alvar's finger touched the hair trigger.

Kenny appeared in front of the Transit, Blair caught in the spectacle. In a nanosecond the back of Kenny's head punctured, blowing out a huge fold of blood and brains which splashed up the windscreen, his ragdoll body bouncing off the bonnet. Cain leapt for cover in the grass as the Transit's wheels span, the back end flailing, before the van lost itself into the foggy plume. Blair's foot was hard on the accelerator, head low, expecting incoming fire, praying the fog would split, which it did, revealing a gate post which stopped the van and sent Blair's head smashing into the windscreen.

Amidst the smoke and chaos, a grenade exploded under the Damascus van. Beyond the smoke a Tec-9 cracked in short rallies, *trrk, trrk, trrk*, Alvar switching it up, Cain's soldiers retaliating with sporadic fire. Eric couldn't see shit. He turned and saw the edge of the Mercedes van and ran, throwing himself against the right rear of the vehicle. *Trrk, trrk* and tight groups of holes sprayed around the cab like lightning strikes, peppering the steel shell, destroying the windows. Eric turned as it came again, *trrk*, a shot ripping through his left arm, sending him rolling in agony, screaming in pain, blood splattering down the side of the van. He crouched down for a moment, breathing hard, then looked over through the lifting smoke of his crashed Transit. Its door opened and out stumbled Blair, disorientated and blinking. Eric charged at him furiously, medieval-like, sprinting, raising his pistol, firing two shots into Blair's chest as he passed him at close range. *Pap, pap!*

The passing momentum threw Blair's legs up in the air, his body pushed back with the impact. He landed with a thud, smashing out the last of his breath, spreadeagled in the dirt. Eric slid into the side of the Transit, skidding into it on his left side. Eric screamed, his left arm an agonising, bloodied mess as he pushed his pistol into his jacket pocket and wrestled to open the driver's door with his right hand. He reached over and slammed his door shut, reversed on hard lock, head down. Brake, clutch. He glimpsed up through the smoke, guessing his exit as he took it out of gear, before thumping his slimy shoe back down. Slipping off the clutch, he crunched the Transit into first, spraying up wads of muck onto the spent bullet casings, blood and bodies.

Cain approached the Mercedes low and slow, creeping around its perimeter, opening the driver's door. He slipped in. No keys. He punched the steering wheel. In the rear-view mirror Kenny's body lay twisted in the furled soil. Keys. Crawling over, shots fired out and Cain dropped in the dirt for a moment as he heard someone running, breathing heavy. He pushed up with his hands and continued crawling, spitting mud, his eyes screaming obscenities.

He got to Kenny and turned him over, diving his dirty hands into the dead man's jacket. Front-right pocket; jingled. Cain grabbed the keys out, keeping low and turned away from the body, placing his hand on an AK-47. Cain's eyebrows raised. He crawled back to the Mercedes, the homeward stretch, like a soldier at bootcamp. He had this.

He chucked the AK on the passenger seat and fiddled to get the Mercedes key in the ignition. He turned the wagon around smoothly and stepped on the gas as he looked up into the blinding, full beam of a car racing towards him. Retinas blown out, Cain jammed on the brakes, smashing into the side of the old Volvo which skidded to block the Mercedes escape. Cain whiplashed back and forwards cracking his skull on the steering wheel.

Frozen in a moment of miasma and white out, a cannon blasted the windscreen twice, raining splinters of glass over him. Cain threw himself into a foetal position across the seats, on top of the AK-47. He took several breaths through gritted teeth, jacking himself full of oxygen.

Per stood behind the Volvo, cocking the Magnum.

"Favorite killing machine!" Cain rasped to himself, pulling the assault rifle around between his legs, cocking it.

The cannon fired, *bam, bam, bam,* inches above his head.

Cain recognised the distinctive sound of the Magnum and reckoned this arsehole only had one more round.

Cain wound down the driver's window, grabbed Kenny's map from the footwell and held it up. *Boom, click* and the map disintegrated, shreds of geography floating down on the sweating captive. This guy was gonna get it. Cain pulled the door catch and slipped the AKs muzzle out the window, turning it to the CLINT behind the Volvo. Squeezing the trigger, the low frequency thud of the killing machine tore through the box-like Swedish car.

"Alvar, where the fuck are you?" Per screamed to himself as he poured the empty shells out of the hand cannon. He dropped six fresh bullets into the cylinder from a Speedloader and felt his body tighten as the AK-47 blasted again, continuing to puncture and lacerate the Volvo's roof.

His next move had to be the kill shot, Cain

knew it.

Per closed the cylinder carefully as he shuffled back, taking in the trim of his wife's well-kept Volvo. He'd enjoyed driving it for over a decade and not given a shit about it. She absolutely loved it. Now it was a right-off. *He's gonna pay for this!* he thought, as he reached the nose of the car, orbiting the AK-shooting motherfucker so he could blast him in the side of his face, in three, two, one …

Per stood up at the head of the car ready to blast Cain at the driver's door. Cain was waiting in the middle of the cab, and before Per could re-aim, the AK was dead on him. *Poom, poom, poom* spat the AK, its muzzle flashing bright orange. Per felt the force of a sledgehammer hit him in the stomach as he let a shot off, falling out of sight of his nemesis. Per lay clutching his wound, writhing like he'd been stung by a wasp the size of a walrus.

Cain had recoiled at the Magnum blast and stood back on the driver's side footplate, maintaining a visual on where he imagined that little CLINT lay bleeding out. A small bird whistled next to Cain's ear, and as he turned Alvar clubbed him across his left orbit with the stock of his sniper rifle.

CHAPTER THREE

LIVERPOOL
Present

Mal carved out an ominous silhouette on the motorway bridge. Looking down, headlights shone through the spray, the cars rooftops a multicoloured Tetris in the darkness, ready to form a solid line. He'd been here every night, reliving a nightmare in a nightmare. He could lean right over the abyss and never fall. Sleep was purgatory and it started with the Shamen, 'Naughty, naughty, very naughty!'

Mal closed his eyes, from one reality to another, the wipers on full as the Ford Escort RS parted the rain at a constant seventy-four miles per hour, Linda and Jackie singing 'Ebeneezer Goode', their clubbing kinship keeping the night alive.

Linda drove, concentrating, but having a good time, her golden waves of hair caressing her face, while Jackie's hips were still in Haçienda mode, rocking left and right, her dark curls bouncing in time to the beat.

"Tuuuunnneeee! Takes me back to Tenerife," Linda said, turning to her friend, giving her a radiant smile before checking her watch. "What time you picking up Little Al?" she said.

"Sandie's got him until tomorrow. The night is still young, babes!" Jackie beamed brighter.

Pairs of glowing red-peppered lights strung out ahead, and Linda slowed to a stop.

Jackie offered her friend a ciggy, and pulled out her cheap blue lighter with a palm tree on it.

Linda smiled as the lighter ignited. She took a drag. "Tenerife," she said, tapping the lighter on the fag packet, blowing out smoke, her eyes blissfully narrowing. Jackie smiled at her friend and that was it. Black. Mal blinked, unable to breathe as the Escort was destroyed with meteoric power, the forty-four-tonne lorry annihilating the car, reducing it to a two-foot chunk of mangled metal.

Mal bolted upright in terror, gasping for oxygen, returning to reality. His bandaged and bloodied wrists throbbed as rain hammered the window. Mal paused, the sound of his pounding heart in his head replaced with the thumping on his front door. Mal looked at the window, hopped out of bed and pulled on some tracksuit trousers. He moved the framed picture of Linda on his sideboard and picked up his pistol.

"Who is it?" Mal asked looking through the peephole.

"Me," said the hooded figure stepping forwards, lowering his hood.

Mal opened the door.

Mal's mouth opened, lips tried to form a question, but nothing came out. "I heard you were dead!" Mal exclaimed, holding his friend by the shoulders.

"No cigar, boss," Blair replied.

Mal pushed the UFC 5 VHS cassette in and it autoplayed; Royce Gracie straddling Ken Shamrock in the Octagon. Blair got a haircut, sitting still, his eyes on the intense grappling. Occasionally, his eyes bounced to Mal's old bodybuilding trophies and photo montages from Mal's past life: training, eating and posing on stage. Mal had had a whole different life before they teamed up. Since Blair had left the army four years ago, Mal and Blair had become inseparable, distributing ecstasy for the Dutch mob into every club in Liverpool. Between the clubs and Mal's salon business, which he'd inherited from Linda, Mal had a machine-like process for turning party pills into clean cash. Mal had picked up other skills, too, giving Blair a new look using a comb and razor as Blair described how he had become a ghost to the Dutch mob.

Mal stopped, holding the razor aloft: "I can't believe I got you this gig and you let a woman compromise everything."

Blair blurted a rapid reply: "I signed up to sell some guns, not … young girls. The army may have fucked my head up, but it took this shit-show to remind me I still got an ounce of moral fucking fibre."

The epiphany had come like lightning strikes in his head.

Blair heard the promise he'd made to the girl in the back of Eric's van. He'd fucked that up. Caspar had nearly shot him with Mal's gun. Little Al had hugged him so tight he'd had to tap out, and then the next thing he was wheezing for breath in a muddy field. Laying there, hearing Sandie tell him "that all the money in the World wouldn't make him a good man," looking straight up, literally seeing stars. Something had to change.

Blair continued to Mal "After Eric shot me, I had a moment of clarity … Bam, bam, bam, bullets flying over me, I realised, once a-fucking-gain I'm fighting somebody else's war. I thought, screw that, I'm out."

The big man stopped again, "Wait, I'll speak to my contacts in the 'Dam. I'll sort this out."

Blair turned to eyeball Mal. "No, no you won't, you're not listening. There's no going back, and even if I did, you know I'd fucking shoot that fucker, Eric, and … that, that wouldn't play well for you now, would it?"

Mal held the razor and comb. "Okay, what are you gonna do?"

Blair looked in the mirror in a cold sweat. Mal paced, eyes locked on to Blair.

"Go where the grass is greener. No more tribes. Get back my ... my purpose," said Blair, double-tapping the UFC fighters on the TV screen, bringing his eyes up to Mal.

"You? A cage fighter? Fucking hell! You're off your fuckin head!"

Blair turned to Mal and put his hands on his hips. "I heard there's a couple of Brazilian fighters who teach world-class grappling in California. I'll master my groundwork, then ... I'll kick some fucking ass! YOU know what it takes to be the best!"

Blair pointed to the bodybuilding trophies on the mantelpiece. Mal put down the razor and comb and pointed to the door, walking in slowly, nodding at Blair.

Blair stood there a new man: goatee shaven to a small moustache, his barnet in a crewcut, rubbing his head and chin. "Alright, cowboy, before you ride off ... I just need *you* to drive the pay run for *me* on Friday night. One last gig?"

Blair remained silent and dropped his head.

"You want a wedge of start-up money or not?" Mal pitched. "Come on," the boss's eyes holding Blair to it.

Blair looked at Mal in the mirror. Silence. The corners of Mal's mouth turned up very gently and he raised an eyebrow. "Just driving, and then I'll put you on the 747 myself," Mal directed.

Blair exhaled slowly.

Mal turned to look directly in the mirror, over Blair's shoulder. Blair's reflection confirmed,

"Just driving."

AMSTERDAM

A white van drove through the picturesque canals and alleys of Amsterdam towards Helmersbuurt. The paradox of the city reflected in the van's passenger window. Scantily clad prostitutes stood, framed, waiting for their next John, next to cafés packed with tourists, sat at round, silver coffee tables, relaxing and smoking joints. The ups and downs, next to the highs and lows, slavery and liberation standing back-to-back.

In the back of the van, pairs of bare female feet touched lightly on the cold, dirty, metal floor as the van rocked about.

At a set of lights, the van paused behind a limo, from which a chauffeur opened the rear door for a suited businessman who stepped out of the car to be greeted at the gang plank of a canal boat by a younger man with a scruffy goatee, immaculate white shirt and silver-grey slim trousers.

The van pulled off the street, across gravel and into an open, dimly lit warehouse. The metal roller door came down swiftly, trapping the vehicle inside. A female foot pointed a big toe, painted red, which touched down as the van stopped.

A large man with a pistol ushered the five blindfolded young women from the van and lined them up under spotlights.

A man in a mask with black and white wavy lines on it sat waiting in the half light. The mask was psychedelically hypnotic and uncomfortable to look at. Next to the masked man, Eric sat, his injured arm still strapped up in a sling. Eric was the only one who knew the man's identity: Harry van Zyl. Eric turned to Harry and winced, the tight black rings of the mask creating a moiré effect that made him nauseas. He whispered something to Harry, who then addressed the shivering women.

"Hold your hands out, palms down," Harry instructed in a calm but chilling tone. He inspected each of their hands before singling out number four: Jada. Harry motioned to the gunman, who turned the other women away and led them out, trailing like paper dolls, arms linked over shoulders.

"Smile. Show me your teeth," Harry demanded. Jada nervously complied. Her teeth seemed normal.

"What is your name?"

"J— Jada," she stammered.

"Take off your jeans, Jada." Trembling, she dropped her jeans, her red toes pushing them to one side so she could cross her legs, attempting to cover her near nakedness. Harry removed her blindfold and she squinted at the sudden light.

"Who are you?" Jada asked.

"God. The Devil. You can call me Boss," he replied cryptically, then whistled, motioning to Eric.

Harry took a step back and Eric knelt before Jada, placing her foot on his thigh. "Okay, hold still, I don't bite," he said, attaching an electronic tag to her ankle. Standing slowly, Jada could feel the man's breath up her body until he made eye contact with her. His eyes drilled her.

"This tag has a GPS tracker. Try and leave the city... you're dead," he warned ominously. Jada had never felt more terrified and alone.

LIVERPOOL

In his studio flat, Blair paced about, the digital clock read 5.24 a.m. He picked up a maroon Sharpie and circled 'Drive' under Friday on the calendar, flinching as his burned hand throbbed. He sat on his bed, still in his black work clothes, and lit a final cigarette, screwed up the pack, and sat grimacing as he applied aloe vera to the wound. He took a long drag and rested his foot on his knee, bouncing it as he scanned the plane ticket. LAX, Monday. Unfolding his wallet he took the photo of himself with Nina out, tore down the fold between him and his ex, opened his Zippo and ignited her image. He held it a moment and placed the fiery mess in a large glass ashtray. He remained holding the other half of the picture, staring at himself in his army fatigues. This wasn't him any more, and he tossed it on the ashes of Nina's image. As it burned he remembered something else. Could he leave it? The relationship burned and he counted down from ten, his eyes flicking to his shorts and hoodie. Seven, he slipped off his trousers. Three, he put out his fag. One, he couldn't leave it, it wasn't over. He jumped into his running kit and left the flat, sprinting into the dawn.

*

Across town, the big man knocked about in his empty house. The carriage clock chimed once for 7.30 a.m, and carried on ticking too loudly Mal thought, as he shook out a couple of green antidepressants, downing them with a small glass of water. Dressed in smart black trousers and a shirt that matched his thick head of silver hair, Mal wrote names of nightclubs and times in a notebook with a black decorator's pencil: Voodoo, 2 a.m., Cream 2.15 a.m., Paradise 3 a.m., followed by Harwich, 5 p.m.

On the table sat two bunches of flowers in simple glass vases. Under his notebook, his open passport, a reminder of his chiselled, fiery, younger self. Mal moved uncomfortably and lifted a necklace with a ring from around his neck, he kissed the ring and dropped it back down his front, as his Nokia pinged, 'Outside.'

*

As Blair ran he felt his lungs filling to capacity, his burning, heavy windbags, out of condition. He tried to stay in control, slowing right down to stop at Morpeth walkway, the adrenaline still pumping as he reached his destination. He ran his hands carefully over the old safety railings which lined the embankment and had a perfect view across the Mersey to the Liver building. There it was, the knot, the insignia of the Royal Staffordshire regiment. Blair ran his fingers over it. The knot featured a coil of twisted rope like an infinity symbol, to which Blair had scratched a B and an N in the loops. Blair felt a rush as he felt for his door key and began hacking at the haunting symbol. He'd removed his half of the urban moniker when someone pushed his shoulder. "Wha' are you up to?" said an old, diminutively skinny drunk, who took two steps back as Blair span around, face red, panting and sweating profusely. "Nothing. None of your business!" Blair barked back.

The old man rested on the railing, unfazed, letting out a *pfft!* "Nothing?" he said, turning his head to Blair. "Everything means something."

Blair scratched off the N and felt like he was floating, the clouds and darkness started to peel away. "Well, I'm done now, geezer," Blair said tapping the railing with his key, letting it resonate as sweat dripped from his chin.

"Ya think you're done," the old man slurred tapping his temple, "but can you scratch away what's inside?"

Blair shook his head at the old man's nonsense. "I ain't got time for you," Blair said, stretching out his calves, looking across the river at the Liver Building.

The skinny drunk man didn't move, clearly relishing any human interaction and closeness. The early morning sun was rising and catching his bald head, silhouetting his weak chin as he mirrored the younger man looking out over the river. He pulled out a small bottle of whiskey from his faux leather jacket and took a swig.

"D'ya know about the birds?" The old man said, pointing at the two liver birds on the Liver building.

"What, the liver birds?" Blair retorted in an uninterested tone as he strained at full stretch.

"You know their story?"

"Nope," Blair replied, switching sides.

"Them two birds, they are a male and female liver bird. They're together, but ... they watch in opposite directions. Now, the female one, yeah, she faces away from the city awaiting …" the old man clicked his fingers a few times, "the, the seaman's safe return. Now, the other one, that's … a male. It, er, he looks back to the city to watch over the seamen's families, it does. Now, legend has it that if they faced each other, right, they might, you know, they might mate and then they'd fly away. So, that's why," the old man brought his fists up and pointed his thumbs in opposite directions, before turning back to the vista.

Blair stopped stretching and leaned into the old man, his head tilted. "I didn't know that," he said quietly to the old man. "Are you hungry?" he asked, pulling a tenner from his hoodie pocket.

The old man took the money from Blair's bandaged hand and may well have drunk more whiskey for breakfast. All that mattered to Blair was that he had given the old man an opportunity to get some scran and was now ready to move on with his life.

Fuck Nina, he thought, she could sweat it in Dubai with her husband and stupid kids. After tonight's job, he'd be on that plane to California and a new life.

*

Mal would have driven himself, but Frank was coming in Mal's prized Jaguar XJS. As Frank was now out of the nick he had finally got to fixing up the midnight blue Jag. It was a fucking beautiful motor; the smell of the leather interior always reminded Mal of his sacrifice and successes as a bodybuilder. He'd earned that motor, rep by rep, pumping iron in the gym. That iron palace threw up mixed memories, both a haven and a prison for guys like him, addicted to building their bodies. It was all worth it; leather smelled way better than sweat socks. He couldn't wait to see the car again. It was a crime that his beautiful car had been left in bits for four years since Frank had been banged up. Today he wanted to be driven in style – he had bought his girls flowers and picked up a *Conan* comic for the kid.

Mal shut the front door and turned to see a battered Fiesta XR2 with Frank's voluminous frame filling the driver's seat. "For fuck's sake," Mal let out to himself as he marched with the flowers to the scruffy runabout.

Ducking inside, Mal held Frank's blank, sleepy-eyed expression, noticing the man's wet lips. Mal's eyes flicked down to a half-empty Smirnoff bottle in the footwell. Mal looked up slowly, controlling his anger, the kid's head popping up over his father's shoulder.

"Late night again?" Mal ventured, curtly.

"Nah, the bottle's half full!" Frank's smile stretched out, a twinkle appearing in his eye.

"You couldn't bring the XJS?" Mal had to ask.

"Nah, it's getting there. The body's fine, mate, but it's still got that coolant problem."

"And it will still have a coolant problem if you don't lay off the sauce." Mal tapped the bare, metal skeleton of the front passenger seat. "What even is this? You bloody joker."

"Another story," Frank replied, moving the busted seat forwards so Mal could slide in the back with the kid.

Mal handed over the comic, gently stroking Little Al's cheek. "Mate, you look brand new. Did your dad chuck you in the tub?"

"I'm clean as a whistle!" the kid replied as the Fiesta sputtered, pulling away.

This was meant to be a quick stop, to drop off the kid. The kid, however, was still in the car, next to Mal, reading the comic, unfazed neither by the scene outside nor Conan slicing through the female vampire Akivasha's throat. Mal, however, was on tenterhooks, eyeballing the scene outside Paul's house. Mal's hand was deep in his blazer pocket. Sandie was amped, she stepped in closer to Frank, "Christ alive! The kid's passport is all I asked you to bring." She looked across to the Fiesta and back to Frank, the round-shouldered, half-cut, unit of a guy, swaying indolently. She'd had enough of him – in the week or so he'd been out of prison he'd proved to be nothing more than an annoying, drunken sack of muscle and fat, his disconnected eyes lost in his own world. "Look at me!" she demanded, "I am trying to give Little Al a life." She turned, now toe to toe with Frank. "You can't do nothing for your son, your own flesh and blood. You never have," she said, pointing her finger at the man's unshaven chin.

Behind Sandie, by the side of the house, Mal could see Paul, Sandie's dickhead of a boyfriend, calmly leaning against the side of his semidetached house, one hand behind his back. Mal's fingers felt the barrel of his gun, and brought them back to the grip.

Sandie continued her tirade. "...if you hadn't got yourself locked up and actually been there for my sister..." her eyes welling up, "... maybe we wouldn't be here now, so don't you flamin' test me, today of all days!" Sandie wiped her eyes and took a step back. Paul stood more erect. Mal took his hand out of his pocket and released the front seat catch, ready to throw it forwards and exit the car.

Paul blinked, trying to remove the sweat from his eyes, not wanting to move, looking between Sandie, Frank and Mal in that piece-of-shit Fiesta. His hand was numb from gripping the kitchen cleaver so tight he had to wriggle his fingers and thought how he could run safely with such a huge blade.

Little Al peeped over his comic, Sandie now with wet panda eyes, continued, "I've mothered your boy for three years, like he was my own, so ... *you* get that boy's passport and bring it to the football on Saturday, cos I have paid for a bloody holiday to Spain and Little Al is coming."

Frank, looked up, breaking his silence, "Where did you get money for a holiday?"

CHAPTER FOUR

AMSTERDAM

The frosted glass of the office filled the space with a diffused, flat light. Looking down from the high ceilings, the room was a maze of desks, computers, fax machines and paperwork, split in half by a seven-foot partition. On one side, Harry sat at a desk, a little black book and his mask next to him. The other side of the partition, his accountant sat with a ledger. The lithe accountant pushed his thumb and forefinger across his narrow moustache, preparing to deliver the deeds. "Shipments from Afghanistan arrived. Surinam's paid up and ... I have tracked back the discrepancies to the British ledger."

"Mal's book?" Harry said, standing up and moving closer to the partition, getting closer to the truth.

"Correct. Over fourteen months ... £103,794 is missing." The accountant underlined the amount with his finger as he read.

Harry turned back fast to the table and smacked his hand on the little black book. He swiped it up and leafed through it, stopping on a page with a head-shot photo of Jackie, her bouncy hair and fun-loving smile, so warm and engaging – on the back it was signed 'Love Jackie x'. Harry let out a slow angry breath, finally the day had arrived for Mal. Turning her signed picture over, he found the number and dialled.

"Eric, I need one of your 'friendly' British associates for a job," Harry said.

LIVERPOOL

Mal marched through the sea of gravestones alone, carrying the two bunches of flowers. A breeze was bringing in rain clouds. His black blazer had the collar turned up and he wore a tight scarf, short around his neck. It may have been cold, but he was glad to be out of that crappy little car. *What was Frank thinking?* He'd only been out the nick ten days, but already a shadow of his former, confident self and Mal's right-hand man. At least Blair was going to do the driving tonight.

Mal stopped. The headstone read 'Linda Tanner 1953–1992'. Mal laid down a bunch of flowers and stood up and back to read the headstone next to it. 'Jackie Strickler 1955–1992'. Mal laid down the second bunch, pausing a moment. He lifted up the chain around his neck and pincered the ring between his fingers that was looped through it. Staring at Jackie's headstone he kissed the circle of gold. "Happy fortieth, darling," Mal said, sinking his head, letting go of the gold band she had given back to him. It was a total head-fuck and the pills just softened Mal up in every way. Any misgivings he had about 'his' Jackie getting with his best friend had well and truly been obliterated by the accident and assuaged by the kid's fun-loving spirit, which brought him some joy and solace. Mal looked to the sky and the tiny fragments of blue behind the deep dark, nimbostratus clouds. "Football tomorrow," Mal egged himself on, it was definitely time to get out of here before the heavy weather snuck overhead.

As Mal got up, his mobile rang – number withheld. "Who's this?" He asked.

"It's me. Extra collection from Garlands tonight. Sealed package. Bring it," the mystery caller instructed.

LONDON

Victoria coach terminal was crammed with passengers through which Aitch's head bobbed to the sound of a maraca. The coach to Liverpool was leaving, its doors closed and the air brakes hissed, "Hey, h-hold the door!" he gasped, as he knocked politely on the side of the vehicle. The driver tutted in the mirrors and continued to pull away, looking to check his exit was clear. The big tyres rolled and the 'hot coach smell' filled Aitch's nose. He jumped and grabbed the driver's mirror, smacking his ticket on the side window. "Stop!" Aitch reeled, eyeballing the driver, who jammed on the brakes. Aitch broke a smile, "Much appreciated," he said and slid down the side of the coach with a screech.

The driver was pissed off at Aitch, but as a student he'd run to many a late seminar and experienced worse bollockings from his film studies lecturers. There was no way he was missing this coach. He desperately needed a night away. There had been a tonne of letters and a rather uncomfortable scenario leading to this trip. For now, Aitch was happy to take the driver's dressing down and collapse in his seat. He had dashed from uni straight to the station and the relief of getting on the coach, the prospect of catching up with his Glaswegian pen-pal, Yazz, and having a night out away from his sex-mad housemates sent his exhausted body and mind into shutdown. He relaxed by chewing cocktail sticks. He was on his way. Aitch rolled the small wooden stick around his mouth and found his composure as he ran through a checklist to appease his anxiety. He'd packed muted clothes, dissertation notes, toiletries, toothpicks and Yazz's letter into his small rucksack. It didn't take long before he was asleep – he was whacked.

The coach jerked to a stop and Aitch awoke at Liverpool station. He glanced out the window, his eyes trying to make out anything in the pitch-black night. He got nothing but his reflection, his brown, wavy hair pushed eight ways from Sunday, the dried toothpick poking into his lip. He spluttered the now foreign feeling toothpick out across the scattered pages of Yazz's letter, tidying himself up as he descended the steps to the tarmac. The warmth of the coach ended abruptly as the freezing cold night air shocked his system. Suddenly he felt unprepared for the night ahead, then he saw them.

The two displaced Glaswegian girls stood arm in arm on the empty platform, jiggling in the cold, fizzing with anticipation. It had been two years since he'd met Yazz in Turkey. Tonight he saw her with fresh eyes, taking her in. Yazz grinned at him, her big, frizzy hair framing her small features. She was petite, but almost everything else she did was big. Her body was somewhere in a bomber jacket and her cute, fitted jeans were accentuated by chunky Dr Marten loafers, resplendent with Grolsch buckles. Somewhat in her shadow, Andrea followed with her gentle smile, an affection to Aitch's silly letters, her scarf and short double-breasted woollen jacket and high-waisted jeans conservative by comparison. "Oh, Aitch ya wee love, I was pure dreadin 'ya wouldn't come," Yazz said. The turning to Andrea, "He's proper braw, Andrea, no?" Aitch twitched nervously.

"Nice to finally meet you, Aitch," Andrea said, as Yazz threw her arms around her special pen-pal for a second then held him back at arm's length.

"Is that it? No sleeping bag?" she said, eyeing Aitch's small rucksack.

"I can sleep on the couch," he replied.

"It's no bother, you can have the double bed," Yazz insisted.

"Well, if that's okay?"

"As long as you don't mind sharing it with me and Andrea," Yazz replied dryly.

Aitch looked blank for a New York minute. Yazz blew up with laughter, looking at Andrea, needling her. She turned to Aitch, linking arms with her best friends and walked to the taxi rank. "I hope you're ready for the weekend of a lifetime!" Yazz continued, pulling Aitch in to her.

"Ready ta go clubbing?" she said, raising an eyebrow.

"Can we ditch this first?" Aitch asked, holding up his rucksack.

The black cab screeched to a halt outside a house split up into flats. Yazz held the heavy internal door open and Aitch set his bag down in the darkness. He picked it up again and hearing the maraca like rattle picked out his octagonal plastic vessel of toothpicks. The door clunked shut.

Tyres rolled, lights changed, Andrea crossed her legs and watched Liverpool flash by. Swarms of revellers lined up at venues, some skin was wrapped in plastic and leather skirts, others swamped in denim and reflective Ts. Yazz leaned around Aitch, pointing her head towards a venue. "That's Cream – too fucking busy," she tutted, leaning forwards to the driver. "You know Garlands? It's up here on the right … can you go a bit faster, I'm busting for a smoke!"

Yazz sat back down, as Aitch pulled out a toothpick, "How's your neighbour – Jack?" he asked, remembering the soap opera of her last letter.

"Jack the rocket? Still got him doing all the manly shite around our flat; goes to the shops, fetches our hash, I even talked him into lending us his phone whilst ours gets connected."

"He sounds … pretty cool?"

"Not really, Jack's a pure choker. He's been creeping around Andrea asking what I like to do, where I go, what I'm interested in. He makes me sick, asking pervy questions, so I sat him down the other night and I told him, if he ever tries to shag me, I'll break his fuckin' nose. Yuck, Jack's a dirty boy."

"He is," Andrea offered.

"Sorry I asked," Aitch replied.

Yazz put her arm through Aitch's, drawing him in and looked up at him dreamily. Aitch played along, pretending to faint at her adoring look. Yazz rested her head on his shoulders.

"Your flatmates still shagging?" she asked.

"Like they're the last two people on Earth! God it's made me feel so ... trapped and infuriated!"

"Gross," Andrea piped.

"Don't let them get to ya. Say something," Yazz said, lifting her head askew at him.

"I will, I just gotta write my dissertation without causing a shitstorm in my own house."

"Well, tonight is the ultimate getaway from all your bothers, like."

Aitch smiled and pulled her closer to him, their arms still interlocked.

"Oh, Aitch, it's pure dreamy to actually have you here in front of us," Yazz squeaked.

"Here we go," Andrea said, the cab now slowing to stop outside the pink Garlands sign.

Eleven-thirty, pubs closed, Garlands was busy and filling up fast. In the purple light and darkness, Mal, Frank and Sparkie stood in a fairly tight group. "We all set for tomorrow? Mal asked. " The Ferry is at 5.30 p.m. Extra pick up tonight, here. Sealed package, so... we're gonna need a mule for this run. Keep your eyes peeled for a girl most likely."

Yazz and Andrea sat at a low table watching Aitch return from the bar. Setting down three drinks on a tray with his passport in between them, *Finally,* Aitch thought, his mind suddenly racing. He was finally here in Liverpool with Yazz, away from uni, his dissertation and his stupid shagging housemates. He was winning at life! Aitch pulled out his Marlboro Lights and offered them to Yazz and Andrea. Yazz looked up from rolling a spliff at waist level, unfazed, like this was Amsterdam or something. Aitch tensed up, looking around, expecting to get thrown out at any second. He rolled his toothpick in his mouth. Yazz looked back down to finish rolling. "Relax, Aitch, this does nae bother the bouncers – they're cool."

Andrea patted an empty leather seat. Aitch let out a breath and smiled as he sat.

"You definitely locked your front door, right?" Aitch asked trying to tick off his anxiety checklist.

Yazz leaned across the table, her hand caressed Aitch's chin and pulled out his toothpick as she closed in to let their noses kiss. "It's all cool, Eskimo Joe." Magic filled Aitch's body and he floated back into his seat.

"Now, are you ready for this?" she said, holding up the spliff.

Aitch nodded, smiling as Yazz lit the single skin masterpiece, took a puff and passed it over. Andrea picked up Aitch's passport.

"This really you?" she said screwing up her eyes, holding up the ID to compare it to the young man's face.

Aitch took a lungful, scoffed and grabbed the passport. "It was taken two years ago!" he said, emphasising the eternity of youthful years.

Outside, Blair was parked down the street, waiting; alone again. That was all this was, driving and waiting; stop, go, stop, go. He'd driven the collection run so many times he could do it on autopilot. He wore black clothes and driving gloves, same every time. Today was different; it would be the last time and for the love of Mary his goddamn left hand was on fire, trapped in these finger-sucking gloves. "Fuck it!" he hissed, admitting defeat and pulling off the left glove with his teeth. He felt the welt on his hand sticking to the glove and the blister tore as he yanked it off. Nerve pain hit him in the right temple and he squinted at the shiny blister fluid trickling down his forearm.

Inside the pulsing nightclub Aitch took a long drag on the joint, holding the smoke in his lungs before exhaling slowly. The haze enveloped his head and his body sank into the chair. He held up the joint for Yazz, but she just smiled and pointed at him.

"For you," she mouthed. "Back in a mo', okay?" she continued silently, through the thumping beats.

Aitch nodded, sinking deeper into the

leather seat as he took another hit, watching the patrons, travelling from the dancefloor to the bar and back again.

Yazz and Andrea crossed the club to where Mal and his crew were loitering. Aitch watched as Yazz introduced herself, bursting the crew's serious bubble, the three men exploding with laughter, standing back to enjoy the Glaswegian firework. Aitch stopped thinking about what was happening, he just felt welded to the comfy leather seat, lost in thought, observing the dancefloor massive. They made shapes, shared a space and stared in wonder into each other's eyes in pure ecstasy to confirm that this was indeed really happening.

Hours, or moments later, Aitch checked in with himself and realised he was completely stoned. He must have blanked out again because suddenly he emerged from the back entrance of the club behind Yazz and Andrea. Aitch scrambled to catch up, the cold oxygen fuelling a huge grin as Yazz slipped her arm through his, Andrea linked into Aitch's other arm and they stumbled, laughing, down the dim alleyway. It was at that exact moment Aitch felt totally relaxed.

A second later the shadows of Mal, Frank and Sparkie reached over and past the trio. Aitch's grip on Yazz tightened protectively before she patted his hand in reassurance.

"Calm down, son. These are my pals, they're cool," she soothed.

Aitch chewed at a cocktail stick nervously. "Yeah, yeah, cool, cool ..."

Yazz nodded to her new pals, then turned back to Aitch. "They've offered to take us to a bar that's open until ten in the morning!" she said enthusiastically. Exhaustion pulled at Aitch's features as he squinted to read his watch – 12.38 a.m. He gave out a little sigh and flicked the mangled toothpick to the ground, his arms now like jelly. Yazz and Andrea were already by the Vauxhall Cavalier. Aitch felt weird, but what the F else was he going to do? The mismatched group piled into Blair's car like sardines and that sealed the deal. Blair flicked the lights on and the Cavalier swiftly disappeared into the night.

CHAPTER FIVE

The throbbing beats of Funkatarium's 'Jump' blared as the Cavalier cruised past the neon lights of Liverpool. Blair bobbed his head to the music while Frank, riding shotgun, made some shapes to the rhythmic pulses. In the cramped back seat, Aitch held Yazz neatly on his lap with an unusually casual intimacy. Squished beside them, Mal eyed Aitch suspiciously, perhaps detecting something beyond platonic affection.

"So, Aitch, is Yazz your girlfriend?" Mal ventured.

"No, we're just old friends from a holiday," Aitch demurred, hoping to brush off Mal's probing stares.

Unsatisfied, Mal pressed further. "Are you bent?"

Yazz jumped to Aitch's defence before he could muster a retort. "Aitch is nae flamer, Mal!"

Seeking to dial back the sudden tension, Mal adopted a friendlier tone. "Look, we're sat too close. I didn't mean to be hostile." He withdrew a moment and returned, his voice in quietened engagement. "Do you want an E?" he asked, and from his pocket he produced a baggie of white pills and extended the olive branch to the unsettled lad.

The older, big guy filled out his black leather jacket, his confidence and stealthy manner were both persuasive and terrifying. Ecstasy just wasn't Aitch's thing, though, so politeness would be his escape. "I'm blasted, thanks" Aitch replied, and Mal turned, tight-jawed, to Blair amidst the noise and chatter of the crammed car.

Up front, a restless energy seemed to grip Frank. "Blair, sort out that 'Deep House 94' tape," Mal commanded, "It's in the right place." As Blair groped under seats and rummaged through compartments for the cassette, Frank's thoughts drifted elsewhere, his stream of consciousness pouring forth. "Anyways, bro, Sandie tells me Paul and her are taking Little Al to fucking Spain on Sunday. 'Go fetch his passport!'" he mocked, "I'm telling you, there's no way Paul, that jumped up prick, is taking my son away on his first holiday ..."

From the back seat, Mal piped, "You should take the boy to the 'Dam some time."

"Ah ... I, I gotta get my shit together first," Frank waggled his fat head, smoothing down his small goatee, before remembering the errand at hand.

"Dammit, I can't find the tape!" Blair said, sounding pissy, putting his injured hand back on the wheel, keeping his eyes on the road. "Chill out about Paul, bro. Check the door compartment for the tape," Blair said, regaining his composure. His voice took on a hopeful lilt, "We'll see Little Al tomorrow. Tomorrow, bro, we can watch the game." Frank's head drew up from between his legs, throwing his hands up grasping the yellow cassette. "Gold!" he crowed triumphantly, popping it into the deck, 808 State's 'Pacific State' pumping out.

The eerie bass tune filled Aitch with dread as he began gulping incessantly. Where was all this spit coming from?

The Cavalier pulled over outside the nightclub Cream. While Frank ducked inside the venue, Blair kept the engine running, the beat of the house music persevering.

Back seat, Mal offered Yazz his baggie, "Want another E?"

Yazz looked at Andrea, "Half each?"

Frank returned moments later and exchanged loaded nods with Mal who tapped Blair's shoulder to set the Cavalier in motion again. "Let's go!" Frank commanded, the wingman renewed with purpose, chipper to be back in the fast lane of the Liverpool underworld.

Within minutes, the car stopped again at the Voodoo club. Frank was out and back fast, with nods and smiles, but not fast enough that Aitch didn't wonder what the hell was wrong with just driving straight to this so called 'amazing club' to carry on their night? Aitch was ready to bounce, his mind pouring over some options – he'd put on an act if need be, so he and the girls could split.

Frank turned to Mal, "Sorted," he said, then turned to the driver, "get us on the M62. Madchester here we come, brother!"

Blair put the gear stick of the Cavalier in and out and back into first gear, then peeled off once more into the night, southbound, to Manchester.

The Cavalier charged down the motorway, its occupants riding in varying states of bliss. Up front, Blair kept a white-knuckle grip on the wheel while house music continued its hypnotic pulse. In the passenger seat, Frank was getting lost in the throes of some personal rapture.

"The boy is tense, Blair," came Mal's voice from the back seat, referring to a rigid Aitch.

"Remember Sunday nights, Blair? The Surinams, Blair, eh? The fuckin' Surinams," Mal continued leaning forwards, his hand on Blair's shoulder.

Blair's expression remained stoic, focused on the dark road ahead. "There was always one," Blair muttered cryptically. A spirited smack on Blair's shoulder punctuated Mal's building fervour.

"Those big machete-wielding Surinams!" The two men chuckled grimly at their shared unnerving memory.

Meanwhile in the cramped rear, Sparkie leaned behind Mal's back, knowingly to Aitch and Yazz. "They used to work the doors in Amsterdam," he offered in a low voice.

The Cavalier continued down the motorway, an ominous heath dotted by moonlight flickered past Aitch's view. Blair stared straight ahead, his thoughts clearly elsewhere. Aitch's inner eye, however, envisioned a grisly tableau upon that lonesome scrubland – a lone, black binbag brimming horrifically with his dismembered body parts.

He shuddered at the vivid daydream, tonight's events spiralling out of his control.

The car pulled up to the pulsating Paradise Club, one of Mal's old haunts. Apparently, they'd be straight in and dancing in minutes. Mal stepped out to confer with his formidable former colleagues to get this guaranteed party started. When Mal slipped back into the car, he shook his head. "This place is rammed," he grumbled. "I used to work with these guys – I respect 'em – so I'm not gonna take the piss." He turned to offer Yazz and Andrea an apology. "Sorry ladies, my French is terrible tonight."

Sparkie leaned forwards eagerly. "Don't worry girls, we'll go to mine. Got some skunk that'll blow your minds. We can pick up your car too, eh, Mal?"

The group assented enthusiastically to

Sparkie's plan. All except Aitch, whose stomach knotted at the prospect of downtime with this crew. Aitch reached for a toothpick to allay his nervous fidgeting as the Cavalier peeled off once more into the endless night ...

Despite his reservations about this band of brothers, Aitch was relieved to arrive at Sparkie's modest home in suburban Chester. The family-sized house was unmemorable with its clean, dark, three-piece suite and enormous wooden shelving unit, except for the silver framed photographs which adorned it. Aitch caught the reflection of his eyes in one frame, part of his body in another, and watched the rag-tag group start the party behind him. At least this felt like somebody's house and the normality had a calming effect. Blair and Mal disappeared into the kitchen as Sparkie cranked up the tunes on a Technics sound system. The huge, heavy, silver separates had back lit buttons, dials and a huge, manual EQ. Cutting edge. Aitch relaxed into the clean, comfy couch and had a few more JD and cokes, watching the foam grills of the knee-high Mission speakers vibrate to the dance music.

The girls threw some shapes with Frank for a while, finally pulling Aitch up. The five of them rode out the tune together, eyes on each other, sharing the moment and letting go, until the chaos peaked.

Sparkie flipped the tape to chill tunes, the suburban ravers flopped onto the couches and the chronically thin host brought over a large translucent blue bong. Frank poured half a glass of vodka into shot of coke.

Aitch held his head back on the couch, his warm neck, damp with sweat, on the cool leather couch. He leaned forwards, face to face with Mal, breathing out after taking a bong hit.

"Yazz tells me you do film studies? Watching movies all day? What skills does that set you up for in life?"

"Film studies is … a lot of analysis."

"Sounds like a load of bollocks to me," Mal laughed.

Aitch sat speechless, his options rolling down faster than a fruit machine. Cherries, a red number 7 and a watermelon, oh fuck! He was tired and needed time away from this objectionable oversized meader before saying something that would get him pulverised.

Aitch turned to Sparkie slowly, so as not to appear alarmed. "Can I … use your men's room?"

"We got a bog, mate. Through the kitchen, follow your nose!" Sparkie laughed. Aitch left the room, the sound of his toothpicks in his cargo trouser pocket adding percussion to the chill-out music.

Mal looked over at Blair and nodded to the door.

Outside Sparkie's home, the night air offered

no relief for Mal and Blair as they conferred tensely by Mal's BMW.

"That bird crap on your car, it's meant to be lucky, right?" Blair ventured, seeking to break the tension.

Mal scraped the offending guano from his prized vehicle with an old beer mat. "Only if it lands on your head," he grumbled, preoccupied with weightier matters, and flicked the mat into next door's hedge.

His voice dropped ominously regarding their unwanted passenger. "This Aitch lad's a spare part, but I think we can get Yazz saddled up for the trip. We need to ditch this wanky student on the way back to Liverpool. Got it?"

Blair gave a grim nod, his eyes drifting up to the indifferent moon.

Aitch exited the toilet, slowly closing the door and turned to see something familiar. On the kitchen table lay Sparkie's Sony camcorder. Aitch stopped, turned the unit over, quickly inspected it and laid it back down. He pulled out his current toothpick, before entering the front room. "Nice ... camcorder that VX1, got them at uni." He said to Mal trying to control his speech.

"Leave that alone, it's got a tape stuck in it," Sparkie snapped.

"Tape jam? I've had that before, takes two

minutes to fix," Aitch replied nonchalantly.

"I said fucking leave it mate!" Sparkie's lips went tight, eyes drilling Aitch.

Mal got up to move away from Frank, closer to Sparkie and Aitch.

"Hey! That's the one with Little Al's party on it," he said quietly to Sparkie.

Sparkie gulped. Mal's eyes opened slightly wider and he turned to Aitch.

"Okay, smart boy ... fix it!"

Aitch sat at the kitchen table with Sparkie, who idly oversaw the educated lad's repair whilst he engineered the filter for a joint from the top of a packet of Marlboro lights, rolling it around the end of a small screwdriver. Aitch squinted, adjusting the diopter and powered the device on. Error code C 31 32 flashed on the camera. Aitch turned to Sparkie, "Can I borrow that screwdriver a minute?"

"I'm fucking using it, mate!" Sparkie said, looking at Aitch in disgust, the weed and papers all out, ready to manufacture a three-skinner.

Blair and Mal sat together on the couch in the front room. Blair riding out the clock, watching his brother entertain Yazz and Andrea, their unblinking eyes captivated by what clearly wasn't a prison story. Blair turned his mind to the smart kid in the kitchen and turned to whisper to Mal, the big man distracted with a framed picture.

"What are you thinking? You wanna just

pull over and dump this lad on the side of the road?" asked Blair.

Mal was lost in deep thought, holding the photo frame. "Don't you think she looks like Jackie?" Mal asked. Blair looked at Yazz, comparing her to the framed picture of Jackie in a hospital bed, holding Baby Al, her sister Sandie and Frank sat either side of the proud mum. Sure enough, there was something of Yazz in Jackie.

In the kitchen, Aitch finished screwing the camera housing together and plugged it into the mains. Nothing. Sparkie, mid-joint, took another toke. "Seriously, fix this or Mal is gonna kill you," he spluttered. Aitch picked up the screwdriver and took apart the tape mechanism. Sparkie let out his smoke, eyeballed the lad dismissively and turned his attention away from the smart boy.

Blair joined Frank, and the foursome ping-ponged stories. At the other end of the room, Mal laid back on the leather foot stool, still holding the picture of Jackie, and let his head flop, seeing the world upside down. He could hear Jackie, clear as day, 'I can't do this anymore, Mal. I want to settle down – have a baby, a family.' Mal sat up and turned around to the group, leaning forwards, elbow to knee, peering contemptuously at Frank through his fingers.

Aitch finished screwing the camcorder back together and pressed several buttons to FORCE EJECT the tape. The error code still flashing.

Aitch's face dropped, Sparkie's eyes gleaming pure Schadenfreude. Aitch twitched and gulped. Taking in a fresh breath he unplugged the camera, then switched it on again. No errors. Aitch's face gave a spasm and his shoulders twitched as a burst of adrenaline shot through him. "Bingo!" Aitch exclaimed. Sparkie pushed back his chair, and with a thankless expression nodded for Aitch to take the camera to Mal.

The TV in the front room flicked into life from black to vibrant blue, the SONY logo flashing momentarily before the long takes of Little Al's fourth birthday party played out.

Blair looked at Mal, who sat forwards to watch, smiling. Blair turned to Aitch the other side of him and said quietly, "Nice work, mate." On the TV, Little Al played with the Scalextric.

"Phenomenal, smart boy. We'll watch this another time," Mal dictated. Frank put his hand in front of the camcorder. "Keep it on," he slurred.

"Yeah, come on, Mal, you party pooper" Yazz jibed.

"Listen, if you girls want a lift home, we got to split," Blair interjected. "Anyways, Frank, it's Saturday tomorrow, the football, you can see Little Al then." Blair looked at Mal who put his fist into his palm. Mal nodded to Sparkie. The skinny host helped get Frank's arm around Blair who walked the giant sack of a man to the front door.

"Go home, bro. Sober up, yeah. See you

tomorrow, bro," Blair said patting his brother's shoulder.

"Come on, cuz," Sparkie said, leading Frank to his Corsa.

Blair returned to the girls in the living room. "You done?"

"Just a minute, I took off my shoes somewhere," Yazz replied.

Aitch picked up a framed photo of Blair at a military checkpoint in Iraq.

"Apparently you can get further with a kind word and a gun, than just a kind word alone," Aitch said, and Blair smiled. "What was that like?"

"Iraq? Relentless head fuck!" the ex-soldier replied.

Yazz and Andrea were crawling around on the carpet, looking for their shoes.

"Let's hit the road," Yazz said. "I'll just buckle up."

Yazz presented her DMs to Blair, jingling the Grolsch buckles on the front at him, along with a big stoner smile.

Blair marched back to Mal who stood out by the back of the Cavalier, the other three trailing behind, staggering and laughing. Mal took a black bag and placed it under the carpet by the spare wheel.

Blair turned to Mal, "Where are we gonna bin off smart boy?"

"We're not." And with that, Mal closed the boot.

Aitch stood behind Yazz, zombified. Yazz turned the key to the heavy front door and he wobbled in behind her. She quickly switched on some lamps, and by the time she had turned to welcome her new pals, Aitch had fallen on the giant beanbag, clutching his rucksack in a foetal position and was out for the count. Yazz smiled softly at him then looked up to Mal and Blair, unpinning her hair, "So nice of you to drive us back, da you want to stay for a wee spliff as a token of appreciation?" The two men stood just inside the large main room, Mal with his hands in his pockets, parting his black leather blazer, looking directly at Yazz, her hair an explosion of curls. For a moment, Mal saw Jackie again, he turned away to blink and tapped Blair to his right, leaning casually against the doorframe to sit with him on the couch. "Love to," the big man said. "This must be the cleanest most organised flat I've ever been in."

Yazz tapped the large American-style fridge. "Not really, you should see the crap we stuff in that, the rest we sweep under the rug."

"You two are a right couple of blasé skallies, no offence," Mal said sitting down.

"None taken," Yazz replied. Blair mooched past the couch to the girls' video collection by the TV. Andrea opened the huge fridge, its interior light brighter than the lamps in the room, then turned back holding a can of coke, a bag of weed and a little bag of cocaine. Mal's eyes opened wide. Yazz glanced at Blair, clearing a spot on their low coffee table, "*Dr No's* up there somewhere," she said. Mal stood up close to Blair, looking at the selection of movies. Blair turned to him quietly, "Right, we're done here, yeah?"

"Thanks. Now relax," the big man pulled an envelope from his blazer pocket, put it in Blair's hand and turned to Yazz. "You look different with your hair down. You remind me of a girl I used to know."

Yazz ran her fingers through her long, dark hair as it tumbled freely past her shoulders. "Oh, do I?" she said sarcastically, raising an eyebrow at Mal. "Is that meant to be a compliment?" She balled up her fist. "That better be a yes, or I'll fill you in right now, ya cheeky cunt."

"Yeah, she was nice; feisty too," Mal replied, unfazed.

"Nice?" Yazz scoffed. "Is that the best compliment a man can give?"

"Okay, okay," Mal conceded. "She was beautiful too."

Yazz looked up at him, her eyelids closed and reopened. "So what was the score between you and little miss beautiful, then?"

"Not much." Mal leaned back in his chair.

"She used to date Harry, a mate of mine. She was poor as a church mouse, though, so when I worked at this club in Amsterdam – best fucking club in the city – I got her a job there as a barmaid."

"That's it?" Yazz asked incredulously. "You didn't get together with her?"

"For a little while," Mal admitted.

Yazz felt irked at the thought of Mal comparing her to another woman. "What did your friend Harry have to say about that?"

"Harry? He never knew, never will."

"You snake," Yazz hissed. "What about her, then?"

Mal waved his hand dismissively and looked away a moment. "Jackie? She's not around anymore."

Blair sat silently and counted the envelope of cash while watching *Dr No*.

"I'm off to bed. Feeling a bit gadge, probably nothing. Night, Mal," Andrea said passing Yazz and Mal.

"Night," Mal replied, turning back to Yazz, he nodded at the sleeping Aitch.

"Your wanky student friend's in the land of nod already. Not much fun, is he?"

Yazz bristled. "You just don't know him."

"He doesn't strike me as your sort."

"Aitch is stressed, he's finishing his

dissertation," she said turning to the photo wall. "Ah, this is more like him – when we met in Turkey." She pointed to a photograph on the wall of Aitch. He stood tanned and smiling on a boat in just swim shorts, one foot propped up on a coil of rope, holding the end of it to his mouth like a makeshift mic – Elvis mid-song.

Mal clearly wasn't convinced. "Do you think he'll be up for a trip tomorrow?"

"He's not into acid," Yazz said bluntly.

"Not that sort of trip," Mal laughed. "We're going to Amsterdam tomorrow to have a party. Wanna come?"

Yazz's hazel eyes flashed with excitement at the thought. She had thought she might take Aitch to Pizza Express tomorrow; Amsterdam sounded way better.

CHAPTER SIX

Aitch awoke with a nudge, feeling disoriented, still sprawled on the beanbag. Something was over the top of him. He was on his back, looking straight up. He suddenly realised he was looking up Andrea's short skirt as she leaned over him to grab her keys from a small table by the sofa. Aitch blinked, "Morning!"

"Oh sorry, Aitch," she said casually as she stood back and leaned down to plant a quick kiss on his cheek. Aitch lay motionless, lost for words. "Bye, Aitch!" Andrea called out. "Gotta bolt or I'll miss my train! Pull the door until it clunks when you leave." She paused to give his cheek a playful little pinch and wink, before heading out the door, letting it slam behind her.

Aitch rubbed his bleary eyes, still processing what had just happened with Andrea. Meanwhile, Blair remained fast asleep in the armchair, that chunky envelope on his lap. Aitch shuffled to the bedroom, excited to see Yazz. Instead, all he got were messy bedsheets and a distant floral scent of Andrea's body spray.

"Idiot," he muttered to himself, "where was she?" He made a strong black instant coffee and wafted it under Blair's nose until he jolted awake, reflexively clutching the envelope.

Aitch stepped back carefully, holding the hot mug.

"Making moves like that, I'm liable to lamp you!" Blair growled.

Aitch stepped back cautiously, not wanting to spill the coffee or provoke Blair further. "Easy there, tiger!"

Blair peered around the flat. "Who else is here? Just you and me?"

"Yeah, where are Yazz and Mal?" Aitch asked.

"They were still smoking at 7 a.m. Mal probably took Yazz to a café for some egg banjo. He won't miss the football, though, so we may as well meet up at the rec, unless you want to stay here and watch the *Lone Ranger*?"

Aitch stepped back to Blair. "Um … nah. I made you a … brew," passing him the steaming mug of rocket fuel.

"Cheers, smart boy."

*

The bright sunlight filtered through the windows of Angie's Greasy Spoon Café and made her hungover eyes ache. Yazz could feel her hands trembling and stuck them flat on the table, a symmetrical target for the plate. As soon as it landed she picked up and bit the fried-egg sandwich. Rich yellow yolk dribbled down her fingers. "Ugh, I'm a total bampot," she grimaced. The big man slipped off his black Ray-Bans and slid them across the table to her. Yazz happily popped them on, giving him a grateful smile. Mal gazed intensely at her, his friendly smile lighting up his face. She tipped the glasses down, playing it cool, making light of what was happening between them.

A warmth grew within Mal, the light caught his eye and images flashed in his mind, the sound of the café was replaced by the sound of his nightmares, the screeching brakes of the 44 tonner, the crunching of bodywork and shattering glass echoed through his mind. Mal stood up, violently jerked out of his psychosis, smacked the table, nearly toppling his coffee as his chair scraped loudly against the floor. Mal closed one eye holding up a hand and turning it into a pistol, shooting Yazz.

"Gonna grab a paper, see you in five," Mal muttered hastily before storming out of the café.

Mal took a deep breath and fumbled to unclasp his necklace with the ring on it and shoved it in his pocket next to his Beretta.

The shrill whistle blast pierced the crisp,

autumn air and focused the two junior football teams as they jogged about, chatted and punched each other's arms whilst they waited for the match to start. On the sidelines, a smattering of parents cheered on the players whilst Kermit-sized kids on massive mountain bikes hollered at each other, ignorant of the gameplay.

Blair and Aitch spotted Mal and Yazz standing at midfield and ambled over. Aitch tapped Yazz's arm, motioning with a jerk of his head for her to join him behind the empty goal for a private chat. She skipped after him happily while adjusting the straps of his backpack.

"Where's Frank?" Blair asked Mal seriously, "thought he was picking up Little Al."

Mal shook his head. "Nah, Sandie brought the kid herself," nodding to her at the other end of the pitch, circling next to the other parents like an angry mongoose.

"Bring the noise!" Blair muttered under his breath.

Behind the goal Yazz lit a joint and passed it to Aitch. He took a long drag and looked at Yazz, who was so buzzing she seemed detached from his reality.

"I thought we were gonna spend time together this weekend, just you and me?"

Yazz waved her hand dismissively. "Don't be

such a mungo, Aitch! Mal just took me to a greasy spoon for a breakfast roll." She turned to him. "He was telling me all about Amsterdam and how beautiful it is there." Bouncing excitedly on her toes, she continued, "He's invited us to come to a party at his new apartment. It'll be such a laugh! What d'ya say?"

Aitch scowled, unconvinced by her enthusiasm. "Amsterdam? Excuse me, Yazz, but Mal's got more pills than a bloody chemist."

"Oh, get tae fuck, ya hypocrite!" Yazz laughed. "He said he hardly ever gets ecstasy. Anyway, he's dead cool. Come on, it'll be fun!" She slid her arms around Aitch's waist, spinning him around slowly, gazing up at him adoringly until his face softened.

The whistle blew, and as the gangsters turned to follow the action Sandie sprinted up. "Where was Frank at nine-thirty this morning? And where is Little Al's bloody passport!"

"Morning Sandie," Blair said, standing between her and the big man.

Sandie jabbed an accusatory finger into Blair's chest. "You promised me things would be different when Frank got out. You're a damn liar. I thought you cared about Little Al. You don't. Saturday mornings Little Al is Frank's responsibility." She stood in to Blair. "In light of him not being here, now he's yours."

Sandie shoved Blair Little Al's PE bag as she

took a step back staring at him.

"Not the left hand," Blair said recoiling, opening out his palms, the PE bag hanging from his left thumb. "We're here aren't we?" he continued, then turned his back on her.

Sandie stood back in and turned Blair back around, pointing at him.

"You think you see everything coming. Well, Mr Know-it-all, let me tell you something, Nina was relieved, no, excited you dumped her."

Blair ran his teeth over his dry lips, staring at her inquisitively. "Where's this coming from?"

"When you were on tour in Belfast and one of your outfit got killed on patrol, that twenty-four-hour radio silence ate Nina up. Not knowing if it was you, it slayed her. Time after time. It did something to her. Nina'd been working for Neil for three months before you finished it with her – he was so kind to her, she really had to hold back. They had serious chemistry. You know what, you didn't dump her, you set her free."

Sandie stepped in pointing at his burned left hand. "That still painful?"

Blair looked away from her as Mal turned. "Run home to Paul, Sandie, he's probably twitching at the curtains, waiting for you."

"You are a rude, selfish pig Mal and I—"

Mal's mobile started to ring. Mal looked down as his right hand rose to grab Sandie's face.

His piercing eyes met hers, "Fuck ... off!" he spat, letting go slowly like he was pushing a small boat away from its mooring. Sandie's jaw remained open as she reversed slowly from the predator's gaze, bumping into the back of Blair as Mal answered the call. Blair turned, catching Sandie as she fell back. Her arms flailing, Sandie grabbed hold of him, letting out a shriek, pulling herself up to him, face to face. "Remember," she said, "*you are not the only one* – look after him until your drunken donut of a brother turns up," then turned Blair by the shoulders to face Little Al. Blair turned back, calling to Sandie, who was already halfway down the pitch, "Okay, okay; and a 'thank you' would be nice!"

Mal's head dropped, he rubbed his thumb and forefinger across his eyebrows.

Blair marched over, "What's up boss? Mal?"

Mal looked up slowly,"Someone's tried to kill Frank!"

Mal's BMW came screeching to a halt outside Frank's lock-up, forming an arrowhead with the nose of Blair's Cavalier. As Mal leapt out, Blair emerged from inside the lock-up wiping his blood-smeared hands on his black jeans, his face like stone.

"He's unconscious, breathing really shallow," Blair reported flatly.

Mal nodded, glancing back at the dark

interior of the lock-up. "Right. I'll shift Frank to the hospital with Sparkie. No need to involve the old bill here." His voice hardened with conviction. "This must have been Paul."

Blair's jaw tightened. "Thinking the same thing," he said coldly.

"Go get him."

Aitch and Yazz watched the football, their warm breath like idling car fumes. Yazz's Grolsch buckles clunked as she began to stomp the grass. "My hands are Baltic!" she shivered. Aitch took off his jacket. "Quick!" he said, slipping her right arm into the warm sleeve, enveloping her small frame in a warm, courteous twirl. He brought her hands up to his chin, cupped them and blew gently on them, touching them a moment to his chin and cheek. He held Yazz's hands out between them, face to face, her nails were bitten down to the quick. "You're a cannibal!" he said dryly.

Yazz stuffed her hands in her pockets and held her head down, "If I mess up again, my mum is going to kill us," she murmured. Yazz outstretching her arms to Aitch and he reciprocated, holding each other around the waist. Instantly, Yazz thawed.

All the letters; advice, doodles and silliness – the girl knew she had a confidante, but nothing could truly beat a hug from her friend. Aitch felt the weekend could begin again.

Behind Aitch a delivery van revved its engine and then braked on the gravelly car park with a crunch that made Yazz jump and turn.

"Hey, you two," Blair called out the van window.

"How's Frank?" Aitch asked.

"Sparks and Mal have taken him to hospital. But they left me with a bit of an urgent problem," Blair said raising his eyebrows meaningfully at Aitch. "Fancy giving us a hand, mate?"

Aitch *ummed* and glanced uncertainly down at Yazz who gave him an encouraging peck on the cheek. "Go on, then! I'll watch Little Al."

With a reluctant sigh, Aitch climbed into the cold passenger seat of the van. "See you later, alligator!" he called playfully to Yazz through the window.

"In a while, crocodile!" she responded grinning, poking her tongue out and waving at him. As the van pulled away, Aitch popped his sleeve-covered hands up briefly to wave back, making Yazz laugh. His playfulness reassured her – no matter what trouble was brewing, she could always rely on Aitch.

CHAPTER SEVEN

The bedroom floor was littered with their underwear. Paul groaned and Sandie's eyes closed as she softly panted. Sandie didn't like any noise, it freaked her out in case Little Al was awake.

"Shh!" She tried, between Paul's thrusts.

"The kid's at football! It's just you and me," he rasped quietly. Sandie's eyes did a double-take at Paul and she whooped and flipped Paul over with her leg, riding him until they reached a noisy-ish climax. Sandie rolled off of him, exhaling as she pressed her head against the pillows with a satisfied smile, basking in the afterglow. Even after years together their physical chemistry had not diminished one bit. Paul stroked her hair affectionately.

"Oh, love, that was amazing," she murmured dreamily, tears of emotion shining in her eyes.

Paul felt a surge of tenderness for Sandie in that moment. "Sweetheart, don't cry," he soothed, leaning in to kiss her. Their tender reverie was broken by the sound of a vehicle revving its engine and braking hard outside. Sandie's eyes opened and she sat up with a start, all vulnerability vanishing as her face hardened, unlike Paul who turned back, standing naked in front of her. Her face found her smile again. "I love you ... Paul?"

Paul raised his eyebrows waiting for the request.

"You need to get Little Al's passport back from Frank," she commanded. "I'm done playing games here."

Paul bristled at her sudden shift in tone, "You sure know how to kill the mood." As he got to the bedroom door she said, "Where are you going, babe?"

"Bathroom, I'll get you a tissue. Glass of water? Then clothes, then the passport," he said reeling off the rest of his day.

As Paul rinsed off in the bathroom, anxiety crept into his guts. He splashed cold water on his face and steeled himself with false bravado.

"It'll be fine, just in and out, real quick," he muttered to himself.

Paul slipped on his robe reflexively patting the robe pocket and gathered up tissues for Sandie as he made his way to get a glass of water from the kitchen. The moment he turned the kitchen tap the doorbell rang. Balancing the glass and tissues on the square top of the bottom banister, Paul opened the front door and there was nobody there. He poked his head out to look left, down the road, his eyes half closed from the bright sunlight. Behind him a dark sack was thrust over his head, its drawstring pulled tight turning Paul's lights out. He felt a striking pain in his shoulder and one to the back of his left knee, sending him onto the concrete. It shocked the wind out of him. Sandie's distant voice called out, but Paul could barely breathe, let alone respond. His hands were tied and he was swiftly lifted, carried and dropped, landing awkwardly in what felt like a van. The suspension bounced under his weight, he groaned attempting to get up, but fell back defeated as creaky doors slammed shut and the vehicle sped away.

*

As Mal shepherded Little Al towards his BMW with Yazz in tow, the boy looked around uncertainly. "Are we going to pick up daddy now?" Mal ruffled Little Al's hair reassuringly.

"Your dad asked me and Yazz here to look after you this weekend. We're going to have a blast, okay?"

"Is your mate Frank going to be ... alright?" Yazz asked with a fragile, drowsy concern.

"Don't you worry, he'll be right as rain," Mal replied smoothly.

Yazz yawned, leaning her head against the window. "I'm totally loused, mind if I have a kip in your car for a bit?"

Little Al seemed skeptical but climbed into the back seat. Mal guided a lethargic Yazz around to the passenger side, holding her hand supportively as she climbed in the sun-warmed leather incubator.

"Make yourself comfortable, lass," Mal said indulgently before rounding the bonnet to climb into the driver's seat.

Yazz sat down awkwardly, pulling Jack's mobile from her back pocket. "Oh shite! Can we stop by mine?" She asked. "Sure thing," Mal replied, as he pulled out of the car park, his eyes shining brightly.

*

Aitch gripped the steering wheel of the speeding van as Blair reached across to turn up the stereo.

"Try and see it my way," the ex-soldier said, his eyes unblinking.

Aitch waggled his hand at Blair, "Your way! In no way is helping the same as ... this!"

Blair turned in his seat and spoke with quiet determination. "Look, the nugget in the back knows me, if he hears my voice I'm fucked, so just help me will you."

"Kidnapping is not the same as helping."

"I need to know if this guy put my brother in

the hospital. Just ask him some questions for me. That's all."

Aitch stared straight ahead as the van motored through the countryside. Blair turned to Aitch who folded his arms. Blair exhaled slowly and angrily. "What triggers you man?"

"Count me out, I can't be a part of this."

Blair tapped the indicator, and Aitch stamped on the brakes, the van sliding across the tarmac of the busy dual carriageway layby.

Blair got out and went around to the front of the van, motioning to Aitch to follow. They faced off, insanely close to the constant, frenetic blur of cars, talking loudly above the traffic noise.

"You know what you are? You're all white feathers," Blair shouted, standing up tall, his hands on his hips. "Take it from me; someday, when you're least expecting it, some mean bastard is gonna come screamin' at you and kicking you're damn teeth in," he took a step closer to Aitch, holding his wrist, "and when you're scrabbling around in the dirt searching for your bloody molars, you're gonna wish you learned how to handle shit like this today."

"You think I'm a soft touch, a— a coward? Well … fuck you! I can handle myself," Aitch said, rotating his wrists to break Blair's hold, backing off, pointing at Blair's face.

Blair opened his arms, palms up. "I'm not

asking you to bust him in the chops, just ask him some questions. Just be Michael-fucking-Caine for five minutes, would ya?"

Acting; it got Aitch's interest, made his nose twitch. "Just asking questions?"

Blair nodded. "So you'll help me."

Aitch exhaled and nodded. "Okay."

"I knew you'd see it my way." Blair smacked Aitch's shoulder approvingly. "Atta boy! Knew I could count on you." Blair took the wheel and turned up the stereo and they drove on through the lush countryside. In the back, their captive shifted uneasily against his restraints.

The delivery van drove in through the tall open gates, followed by a small dark canopy of oak trees and up a long drive to a remote Georgian mansion. Blair paused out the front, engine running next to a large, circular stone fountain that seemed to spray diamond-like water droplets. Aitch rubbed his eyes at the otherworldliness of the wealth. "Owner's some American film producer," Blair explained. "Sparks is doing renovations around here."

Blair put his foot slowly on the accelerator and eased the van around the back, past the stables and outbuildings to a courtyard, stopped and turned to Aitch. "Remember, no names. If I need to talk to you, I'll signal you."

They entered the bright white, sparsely furnished room with white curtains over the windows. Drop cloths and painting supplies were scattered about, along with a TV on a tea trolley. Aitch set his backpack down and helped Blair deposit the wheezing Paul onto a chair, which sported a shiny vinyl upholstery. Blair flicked on the TV; golf from Sunningdale. Aitch looked at Blair as he switched the channels to a 'Don't try this at home' stunt show.

Paul sat with the bag on his head, hands tied behind his back in his dressing gown in the middle of the room.

Blair whispered to Aitch, cueing him. Aitch adopted his best Michael Caine accent.

"Where were *you*, this morning?" he began, a loud but steady Michael Caine, enunciating every word.

Paul struggled against his bindings. "Take this fucking bag off and talk to me like a man, you pussies!"

Aitch stayed calm. "Wrong answer."

Blair tapped Aitch's shoulder to step aside and he slapped Paul hard, sending his robe gaping open.

"Settle down, no one needs to see that!" Aitch retorted in an irreverent tone, covering Paul back up awkwardly. "Just tell us where you was this morning, okay?"

Blair grabbed the captive and shook him.

"I was at fucking home. I was at *home* ... plastering a stupid fucking hole in the fucking ceiling!"

"On your own?" Aitch replied.

"No, with Sandie and Little Al ... his dad, Frank, he didn't turn up ... again, so Sandie took Little Al to football. That's it."

Aitch looked at Blair. Blair rolled his hand to keep going.

"What? What's this about?" blurted Paul.

"Tell me about the kid."

"What?"

"You heard, tell me about the kid."

"Al's ... a nice kiddie, but I ... I want his father to take care of him, let me bring up my own family."

Aitch made a T sign to Blair and they conferred behind the TV. Whatever Aitch said, it flipped a switch in Blair, he charged at Paul, lifting him by the throat and slamming him into the unpainted dry wall, stabbing his hunting knife in deep, next to Paul's head.

"No more bullshit!"

Suddenly Paul went limp, wheezing weakly as he dangled. Aitch could see the life drain out of the man's body rapidly and helped Blair sit him back down on the vinyl-covered chair, which squeaked against his bare flesh. "Stab me!" he rasped.

Aitch looked at Blair and raised his shoulders. Aitch pulled the hood off, looking into Paul's wet saucers.

"I'm allergic … to vinyl … EpiPen in …"

"Fuck!" said Aitch, pulling Paul directly onto the cold floor, his body listing to one side, his arms tied behind his back, his lips tasting dust. "EpiPen? Shit! He's having an anaphylactic reaction."

Blair tapped the robe pocket and whipped out the EpiPen. He scooched in close to Paul, "Not a word about this to Sandie, yeah?"

Paul nodded, a wave of relief replacing the look of deathly submission. Blair removed the safety lid of the injector and suddenly stopped to listen, the sound of a vehicle on the gravel outside. Paul gurgled trying to breathe through his spit. Blair hopped up and ran low to the window. Paul's eyes bulging, wheezing through his wet mouth. "EpiPen!" Aitch snapped, thrusting his hand out. Blair looked back and threw the EpiPen to Aitch who caught it and stabbed the injector straight into Paul's thigh. The adrenaline kicked in instantly and Blair quietly leaned in menacingly.

"You didn't see anything, right?"

"Right," Paul said with relief turning to realisation as Blair peeled the hood back over his head.

"It's the old bill!" Blair said, grabbing his hunting knife from the wall, head turned to Aitch as he wrestled the jagged blade out. "Get in the van, wait for me, but don't start her up." Blair grabbed the gaffer tape next to the TV and flung the keys to Aitch. "Rucksack!" Blair snapped, the lad start,-stopped, his heart racing. Aitch had never felt this kind of a rush. His mind felt completely clear, he almost tripped over himself, he was moving so fast. He ran back from the wide ostentatious staircase, past the kitchen, through a scullery to the back door. He stopped. Opened the courtyard door a bit. Nobody. He opened it and danced carefully across the gravel to the van trying to be light on his feet.

He stopped himself slamming the van door, leaving it ajar. Aitch's hands were trembling so much he dropped the keys on his lap. Finally, he got the Leyland key in the ignition. Now what?

Officers Briggs and Hunt approached the mansion's front door across the gravel, finding it slightly open.

Blair appeared in front of Aitch and made quick eye contact at the smart boy, holding up his hand, signalling to wait. He then turned to watch the police from the wall of the courtyard about twenty metres away.

Hunt, fair haired and the smaller of the two, knocked the large brass knocker on the closed door. A knocking noise emanated from upstairs. Blair peeled up the edge of the gaffer tape.

Briggs, the taller officer, took off his helmet and put his dark curly haired head in through the gap in the door. "Hello, this is the police."

"Hell!" an exhausted voice tried. The two policemen looked at each other. "Help!" The voice called again, clearly.

As soon as the policemen stepped inside, Blair turned, waving Aitch on. Go time.

Blair ran from behind the courtyard wall to the open front door, closed them quietly and tacked the edge of the gaffer tape to the door knocker and span it around the other one, binding them together. He left the tape hanging and pulled out his hunting knife, running low past the fountain. He thrust the tip of the serrated blade into the rear and front passenger-side wheels of the police car, *pap, pap*.

Aitch slammed on the brakes as he saw Blair appear in his left peripheral vision and the van stalled, only just rolling along. Officer Hunt wriggled out of a ground-floor window, landing unceremoniously in a rose bush. Blair jumped in the van as Aitch popped it in second gear and jumped it back to a semblance of life, slowly accelerating as Hunt tore himself from the rose thorns and began chasing them down the gravel drive. Hunt's baton pounded the side of the van door, booming metal vibrations through Aitch. The copper gained on them, smashing the driver's window. Aitch flinched and swerved, Hunt looked down and tumbled, disorientated, face first into the gravel.

The van passed the gates, Aitch wrenched the wheel left and the wagon bumped back onto tarmac at speed, his heart pounding out of his chest.

CHAPTER EIGHT

A fog horn sounded. The departures area at the port of Harwich was busy with families and truck drivers preparing to sail to the port of Hook in Holland. As Mal returned to his young companions, holding Yazz's ticket, the PA sounded, "Last call for the 5.30 p.m. Stena Line crossing to Hook. Please make your way through customs, thank you."

"Here's your ticket, lass" Mal said, "We'd better hurry," he continued, then stopped. "Wait. I gotta take Al for an emergency pee. You go on, we'll meet you after customs."

"Nae bother, see ya in a mo," Yazz said, and rolled the green, medium-sized wheeled suitcase towards the checkpoint.

*

Aitch's stern face shook, as angry vibrations replaced the adrenaline high of their escape.

Blair smacked the dashboard.

"I can't believe you took his hood off and compromised us!"

Aitch exhaled. "For fuck's sake, you said we were just gonna ask Paul some questions! You nearly killed him."

Blair scoffed. "I'm not the one who stabbed him with that EpiPen."

Aitch set his jaw. "Look, I did what you asked, but ... that's it. Whatever happened to Frank, I'm sorry, but that ... that's for the police to figure out. Just drop me at Yazz's."

Blair leaned back calmly. "Fine by me ... if you fancy spending your weekend on her doorstep."

Aitch froze. "What do you mean?"

"Yazz is off to Amsterdam already ... with Mal," Blair revealed pointedly.

Aitch clutched at his hair in dismay, running his face down the sleeve of his fleece. "But, but, I gave her my, my jacket, which has ... my wallet in it ... fa, fa, fuuuuuuck's sake!" He swerved the van into a layby, pulling over as wave after wave of shock and betrayal crashed down on him. Head in hands, he let out an anguished growl.

Aitch stumbled from the delivery van, disorientated and heartsick. Blair leaned back against the front of the van in the sunshine and folded his arms, watching the lads aimless escape attempt. Aitch broke into a desperate run across the muddy field, his trainers slipping, legs flicking out, all punctuated by the maraca rattle of his toothpicks. Weak and wasted, the field got the better of him and he fell, faceplanting the dirt, his hands sliding in front of him into a pile of steaming cow shit. Aitch could feel his fingers in the warm, wet muck and shuddered as he slipped them out and wiped them on the grass.

Aitch trudged back miserably, stopping to wipe more muck off on the grass. Blair called out, "You forgot your passport!" holding up the document. Aitch's rage and humiliation curdled into bitterness towards Blair for duping him into this violent fiasco. Aitch couldn't look at Blair as he passed; as he did, the grinning gangster tapped Aitch with his passport, and that was all it took. Aitch snapped. He whipped around unleashing a wild haymaker with a guttural cry. Blair sidestepped the fist and Aitch's momentum sent him crashing into the side of the van. Aitch groaned as the wind was knocked out of him. He peeled his face from the van and turned.

"Woah there!" Blair was right up on him. He pinned the lad's arms using the side of his body, keeping his bad hand out of the action, before Aitch could take another swing. Trembling with adrenaline, Aitch struggled uselessly against the stronger man.

"Cool it, would ya?" Blair said sharply. "We've got bigger problems here." Releasing Aitch, he stepped away to defuse the tense standoff.

Aitch panted heavily, his anger dissipating. "What do you mean *we*? I don't want any part of this shit any more!" He turned and walked a few paces, only to stop short at Blair's calm reply: "You're a free man. Alright, I tell you what? I'll drive you anywhere you want to go in the city." Blair stopped and put his hands on his hips. "Who else do you know in Liverpool?"

Aitch was silent.

"Look, I got your six, now get in!" Blair said. Aitch sighed and they both got back in the van. Blair paused before setting off. "Hey, I'm good company, you just don't know me yet."

Back on the road, Aitch took a few minutes to compose himself before turning to Blair.

"I don't think I want to know you. Seems to me, someone, somewhere, some mean bastard is trying to set you up – kick you about in the dirt, something like that." Aitch looked out the window for a moment, then back to Blair. "Fuck it, let's just, let's just … get my wallet back," the smart boy said in a conciliatory tone.

Blair nodded, "Thank you."

*

Under the toilet cubicle, Little Al's cross-strap trainers and Mal's black leather shoes faced each other. The toilet flushed. "Okay, kid, let's wash those hands."

Standing in the customs line Yazz reached in Aitch's jacket pocket and pulled out his wallet. All her movements slowed down as she held it up, staring at it. She bit her bottom lip and breathed out a silent F, her eyes wide open.

*

On the outskirts of Liverpool, Blair pulled into a driveway of a reasonable-sized detached house. It was tucked away, with lots of bushes and green cover. He drove around the back, hopping out to punch in the code to a keypad which operated the large blue steel gate. They parked in the large secure yard and Aitch got a weird vibe about the place. The back of the house had a huge pre-fab building made of solid cement slabs, with two double garage doors on the back of it. "This is Mal's place," Blair said.

*

As the ferry pounded its way through choppy grey waves, Little Al sat on a deckchair, watching England disappear. Next to him Yazz stood with Mal having a tête-à-tête. She leaned over the railing, her face, untypically introverted. "Aye, I feel like such bampot skulking off with Aitch's jacket – I hope he's not raging at me." Trying to justify her impulsiveness, she turned to Mal, forcing a smile. "I'm buzzing to get away, though, y'know? Change of scenery and all that," Yazz said. She reached over and touched the big man's arm. "So, Aitch and your man Blair'll be over later, yeah?" she said, screwing her face up, squinting at Mal, trying to make herself feel better and appease the big man. The answer came by return as Mal smiled back indulgently with a little nod.

"Party time!" He saw Yazz and Jackie intermittently, their faces blurring reality with his memories. Having Little Al here too, somehow made him feel complete. She was the light to his darkness. She could fill in the blanks, bring back the old Mal. He could feel her looking at him, he turned and rested his right arm on the rail, opening himself up to her. "Of all the places, why'd you move down to Liverpool, lass?" he said.

Yazz looked at her feet a moment, some colour came to her face as she replied in a matter-of-fact way. "Since my brother Graham moved down tae London, I got into a wee spot of bother driving my mum's car, an' doing too much eccie. Car was the last straw for her, though, it's her pride an' joy."

Mal raised his eyebrows. "What's she drive?"

"Peugeot 205 Roland Garros special edition; yeah, it's pure gorgeous, with white leather interior. She was away in India, where she's from, like, so I used it. I have nay got my licence, but I'm a good driver."

"Oh yeah?" Mal said

Yazz kind of shrivelled up, her teeth against her lower lip. "I sorta parked it intae a lamppost, so I did. Cost six-hundred quid tae fix it. Got it home, fixed, twenty minutes before she came through the front door. Proper heavy."

"Did she suss it," Mal said.

"I was dead paranoid she'd find out about the bump. I started smoking loads more hash than usual. Ended up, she caught me wi' a joint and an ashtray full a roaches. She was pure screaming at me about the hash and ... I lost it, fessed up about the car. She thought I needed to get away from Glasgow, so me and Andrea moved to Liverpool. I tell ya, honesty gets you nowhere," Yazz concluded glumly, shivering against the chill wind.

CHAPTER NINE

Blair walked through Mal's storeroom, the tube lighting flashing on. Aitch followed, the blinks of light illuminating the horrific amount of stolen electrical gear that lined the walls of this maze-like rabbit warren. The racks of inventory opened out to a delivery area with floor-to-ceiling roller shutters. Just beyond that, the huge storeroom had a shelving unit which sectioned off a makeshift living room area, with a sofa, table and a giant CRT TV. Behind this area was a kitchenette on one side and an enclosed office on the other. Blair gestured impatiently to the makeshift kitchen and didn't look back. "Make us a brew, yeah? Need to make a quick call."

Aitch filled the kettle as Blair entered Mal's office, his outline blurred through the large, frosted windows.

In the office, Blair bobbed impatiently holding the telephone. He listened carefully, a pencil stressed between his fingers. He took some slow breaths. "No refunds? You gotta be … fucking kidding me!" There was the sharp crack of splintering wood, as the pencil snapped.

"Fuck it!" he said kicking the wheeled desk chair across the office into a metal cabinet with a hollow boom.

A picture frame toppled down and smashed on the floor.

Aitch turned, but the frosted glass gave nothing away, holding Aitch in suspense. Aitch opened the fridge and turned the half-empty milk bottle, sniffed it, squinted at the stench and poured the sour milk down the plughole.

Blair got down on his knees and turned over the broken frame, looking at the photo of Frank and Little Al, the glass splintered between them. Blair exhaled and held his head in his hands. He bobbed his head in affirmation, then jumped up, opened a cupboard and changed from his joggers, hoodie and trainers into some jeans, a jacket and a pair of combat boots.

Finally, Blair opened the office table drawer, removed a pistol and deposited the plane ticket, slamming it shut.

"Stay!" Blair instructed and shut the drawer.

A different version of Blair appeared as he marched back to Aitch. "Change of plans," he informed Aitch grimly. "Whoever attacked my brother could be back to finish the job. I need to get to the fucking hospital."

Aitch nodded and wordlessly passed him

the steaming mug of black tea. "Milk was off," he said. Blair set it right back down, shaking his hand reflexively, his stormy eyes simmering. Vengeance rising.

Aitch looked down, taking a moment from the stare, getting the right oxygen. He looked up, "But ... wait, what about me? Amsterdam? I gotta ... get ... my ... wallet?"

Blair cut him off sharply. "Sack Amsterdam!" He said, standing into Aitch. "Look, I don't trust anyone else. You're a smart lad, stick around, help me figure out what the fuck is going on, yeah? Be an extra pair of eyes for me until tomorrow night and when Yazz returns with Mal, you'll get your wallet back and then you can put this in it."

He slapped his now beaten-up envelope stuffed with cash into Aitch's confused hands.

"Wow, What's this?"

"That is a royal goodbye to a new life in California." Blair turned away, holding up his watch.

"I don't think I can help you and I don't want your money!" Aitch said slowly, gobsmacked by the offer. He protested in dismay, "I just ... need to know Yazz is alright." His eyes widened. "I'm worried about her, okay? Yeah, I'm worried, I don't mind telling ya." Aitch felt a rush and paced about.

Blair stood in front of Aitch, hands on hips. "Stay calm, mate, have a toothpick. Think about it for half an hour. I'm going to the hospital to make sure no fucker gets to my brother. You hold the fort here and let Pie and Gibbsy in with their delivery."

Aitch felt his pockets for his toothpicks and by the time he looked up, Blair was gone.

"Who are Pie and Gibbsy?"

Aitch paced the warehouse storeroom anxiously, then threw the envelope on the table, sat and counted it – £5,450. His lips were dry as he blew his scalding tea. It was too hot. He tried to gulp but his throat was bone dry. Aitch began stirring the undrinkable liquid with his toothpick, administering single drops into his mouth.

Trying to calm his nerves, he sat, looking around this Aladdin's cave of stolen gear; everything from nicked car stereos to cardboard boxes of new electrical products and shrink-wrapped items. His eyes finally settled on a pile of designer clothes laid out neatly on a seat next to the kitchenette. Aitch sighed and then looked down at his backpack. He was on his own and for once it was quiet. *If Blair is sorting out his business,* he thought, *I'm getting on with mine.* The bloody dissertation wasn't going to write itself. Aitch got out his array of photocopied pages and paper, composed himself and with his first sentence forming in his mind, *knock, knock, knock* went the front door. Typical! He put his tea down on the kitchenette side and went to see what inconsiderate numpty was disrupting his education.

Peering out the spyhole, Aitch took in the sight of an AA patrolman, a short, lithe chap in bright yellow coat and red Doc Martens. The little chap spied the spyhole, behind him a bright yellow AA transit van. Inside, a scowling beanpole of a man with an arm in a plaster cast took a long drag of a cigarette.

Aitch hesitantly opened the door, craning his neck to assess the unexpected visitors.

"Watcha," the little chap said, "Mal about?"

"N— no."

"What about Blair?"

"He's ... popped out, sorry is this a ... personal visit?"

"Nothing personal." He turns to the man in the van, "They're both out, Gibbsy."

The lanky chap, now out of the van, threw his fag on the tarmac and motioned Pie to get on with it.

He turned back to Aitch. "I'm Pie, by the way."

Aitch worriedly rolled his toothpick to the other side of his mouth. Pie marched in, throwing down his jacket like this was a home from home.

*

Inside the hospital room, Blair clasped Frank's limp hand. A doctor stood the other side of the bed holding a clipboard, obscuring Sparkie. "We've sedated your brother and he's on a drip in an induced coma to help relieve the swelling. He'll be in here a few days at the very least." The doctor's eyes met Blair's and he flashed a token smile, flipped his papers back over his clipboard and left the room. Blair's face slowly contorted in anguish and rage, his foot tapping, and then turned to Sparkie. "You okay to watch over him tonight?"

Sparkie lifted his jacket just enough to reveal a pistol tucked into his waistband.

*

The roller shutters opened. Pie wafted for Gibbsy to reverse into the delivery bay. Aitch watched from the kitchenette. The van stopped and Gibbsy got out. Pie opened the back of the AA van and was faced with more rows of neatly stacked boxes of electrical equipment. Aitch watched nervously and slowly crept forwards to idly peruse the haul.

"Fucking hell, Gibbsy, give's a hand with this!" Pie called.

Gibbsy jumped out of the van, facing off with Pie, like a boxer at a weigh-in, then stepped back, his bloodied fingers holding his watch. Gibbsy turned to Aitch, then back to Pie, holding up his bloodied plaster cast.

"Nah, cos of *you* I've got to clean this off, so *you've* got twenty minutes to get *this* lot unloaded. Get your new mate to help." He shoved Aitch roughly towards Pie, who piped up, pushing several boxes into Aitch's hands.

"These boxes go over on the left by the widescreen tellys," Pie directed, piling Aitch's arms high with DVD players. Overwhelmed, Aitch scurried to comply while Pie supervised lazily, chain-smoking cigarettes.

"Hurry up, I got to get the fuck out of here, pronto!" he said, always ready with another box before Aitch returned.

"Move it, let's go, dickhead!" Pie snapped as Aitch struggled under the weight. He picked up Aitch's backpack and carelessly tossed the remaining notes on the table. "What's all this shite?"

"Oi, careful!" Aitch protested hotly, "That's my dissertation."

Pie scoffed. "You're a student?"

"I *was* meant to be spending this weekend with … an old… girlfriend, not to mention I've got to have … *that* finished and handed in on Tuesday."

"Ha!" Pie put down his box and lit another cigarette. "Sorry, where's ya girlfriend?"

"She's had to go away this weekend … with Mal," he admitted.

"Err, and you're 'ere! Look out, Cilla. Surprise, surprise!" Pie laughed and took a long drag.

"What do you mean?"

"No one knows Mal better than me. Every time I do a job for him, he's off with some other bint."

"A bi— Yazz is not a bint!" Aitch exclaimed coldly, as Pie took a drag of his cigarette, the tattoo of the tree swallow on Pie's neck pulsed angrily. Balling his fists by his sides Aitch fought to control his frustration.

"Really? If your 'girlfriend' has copped off with Mal, what does that say about her?" He said, blowing smoke in Aitch's face. Upstairs the toilet chain flushed. Aitch turned and took another dry gulp.

Gibbsy zipped himself up with his plaster cast hand and stood in the almond-coloured bathroom gelling his short, cropped hair in the oval mirror. He'd chucked his used towel in the bath, ripped off the clothing tags and dropped them on the floor. He stood admiring himself; Ralphy shirt with one sleeve rolled up, Armani jeans and white Reebok classics. He grabbed his packet of Lambert and Butler silver and stuffed them in his jeans pocket. Class.

Pie sat back, splayed on the sofa with his Doc Martens on the low table, his fag like a hot poker pointing at Aitch. "Relationships with women never last. My five kids, though, they're solid, like trophies – something I can be proud of." He exhaled. "Hard work supporting them."

Aitch felt a sense of revulsion, this little chap, this cheeky fucker, had bossed him about, got his hands dirty humping about stolen gear.

"Hard work you mean ... this? Stealing?" Aitch said dryly.

Pie sat around, putting his feet on the floor, symmetrical, stubbing out the remnant of his cigarette in a now full Wadsworth's ashtray. "Look, it isn't like, me and Gibbsy mug old grannies. All this, *this* is overpriced, production line bollocks from China that we nick from larger high-street shops. And as it goes, I always need four of everything, for me family," he said in a matter-of-fact way.

Pie sat back and lit another fag.

"Okay," Aitch said slowly, his hand still by his side, fist clenching and unclenching.

Pie rose up and came forwards again towards Aitch. The veins in his neck came up and drew attention to the bird tattoo which Aitch could now see had song notes emanating from it.

"I got my own laws, sod the rest! Britain's for the British. Look around ya, we're flooded with technology from the far east. Gibbsy and me, we're just mopping up the excess. I mean ... you can't watch British TV on a British TV anymore, or eat British food when you go out. Fuckin 'Sony this, Hitachi that, Chinese, Korean – whatever! See I'm not stealing for me, or for the money ... I'm stealing for England!"

Aitch held Pie's stare. "Ferguson ... is a British TV manufacturer."

Pie's expression turned from smugness to rage, without a breath, stepping over the low table bringing the heat to Aitch. "What did you say, prick?"

It caught Aitch off guard and he stumbled backwards, knocking his hot tea over Pie's folded new clothes and trainers. Pie lunged, sweeping Aitch's legs out from under him with a kick to the ankle. As Aitch sprawled on the floor, Pie snatched up his soaked clothes and stood firmly on Aitch's ankle. Then he hurled the dripping bundle onto Aitch's chest.

"You've fuckin' ruined these!" Pie snarled, snatching up Aitch's notebook from the table. "How do you like me now?" he said and lit his Zippo, bringing it slowly under Aitch's dissertation notes.

"No!" Aitch yelled, twisting his leg and tripping Pie. Pie crashed backwards, the back of his head smacking the metal shelves. Scrambling to his feet, Aitch stamped out the burning pages and fled through the maze of boxes, Pie scrambling up after him. Ducking behind some racks, Aitch caught his breath – until a tap on his shoulder made him whip around, the adrenaline and survival instinct, kicking in, he drove his fist into Gibbsy's gut. Gibbsy wheezed, folding in half.

Pie was approaching fast. Aitch ducked and turned, and then at the last millisecond and Pie was thrown over Aitch's back, barrelling into the winded Gibbsy. Aitch lost his balance and fell face first on the floor. Aitch turned over, grabbing the ankle Pie had smashed into and looked up, frozen in terror. The two men loomed over him, righteous fury etched on their faces.

Gibbsy stopped wheezing and looked down, staring at Aitch, then pulled something from his pocket. Aitch heard the flick as Gibbsy's blade opened and the lanky guy put his other hand out to stop Pie. This was his fight.

Aitch started to move backwards on the floor, like a spider that's missing a leg, and got himself on his feet. Gibbsy stepped forwards, swiping left and right with the knife. Aitch hopped back, the knife slashing his fleece. Aitch glanced to his left, there was a stack of car stereos, the top one had a handle and Aitch grabbed the little metal box. He swung it across Gibbsy's next swipe of his flick knife. Gibbsy's arm flung up in front of his eyes and span him off balance, facing away from Aitch. Aitch pushed Gibbsy's button arse, launching him into the racking. With a clear path to Aitch, Pie ran at the adrenaline-fuelled lad.

Aitch whipped his arm and wrist and let go of the heavy metal box, which smashed Pie directly in the forehead, dropping him with just a squeak as Pie's chin burned across the lino floor.

Aitch felt a hand on his back and he jumped out of his skin. Blair raised his eyebrows at the carnage and back to Aitch who was still jacked full of adrenaline, now pacing about in his sliced up fleece.

"You okay?" Blair asked.

"Fucking ... F— fuming," Aitch replied.

Gibbsy got up groaning. He looked at Pie and slowly picked up his knife off the floor.

Blair pulled a pistol from his jacket and cocked it. An ace to a king. Pie and Gibbsy stopped as their eyes met Blair's intense stare. Blair motioned the gun towards the door, like he was flicking a tiny speck of shit off of the barrel. "Get out!"

Gibbsy tapped Pie's arm and they left.

CHAPTER TEN

The two men stood three metres away from her window, smoking, eyeing Jada up. The thirty-somethings caught her eye; clearly idiots on a stag do, wearing their gold novelty top hats that read 'Best Man' and 'Groom'. They were clearly talking about her, objectifying her, a body for sale. Another day in one of Warmoesstraat's busiest brothels. She wore a basque and a bow in her hair and did what she was told – keep moving subtly to usher in the Johns. Jada's fresh face had been picked by randoms and regulars more than any other girl in the nine days she had been on the game. Now, the smile didn't come naturally. Jada felt flat, her mind blitzed; regular flashes of violation frightening her. Her life, a waking nightmare. It was happening now, her body spasmed and twitched, so she quickly turned to transition her pose and sit in the satin chair. Instantly she felt relief from her aching, pretty feet, unused to the daily wear of high heels. However, sitting on her bits, even on a cushioned seat was the worse of two evils. She was sore and bruised and sat on one cheek to try and keep her bits cool. Every second of this life, she was a slave, disconnected from anything like normal life. Jada watched the two men come closer. The groom put out his cigarette, the best man patted him on the shoulder.

"You're up, Jada!" Marjo called. In her late forties, Marjo had been at the brothel for years and ran the girls under the watchful eye of Serge. Jada tried to stand, and walked awkwardly out to the reception. She looked up at a light behind a spinning fan and the effect made her eyes flicker and she collapsed in a dizzy mess into Marjo's arms.

"I can't do it!" Jada said breathlessly.

"You've got to do it, or Serge will lose his shit!"

"I'm so bruised, it's killing me!" Jada replied.

Marjo looked into space for a second, then reached into her pocket. "Take this, go rest and I'll take your John if you take mine, my foot man in … fifteen minutes," Marjo said as she placed a green pill in Jada's hand. Jada looked at Marjo inquisitively. "He gets off on feet. You'll be fine," Marjo continued.

Jada laid on the messy bed and swallowed Marjo's pill. It felt like an effervescent Catherine wheel in her stomach. What with the dripping shower in the corner of the room she had no opportunity to rest before the inevitable knock at the door. To her surprise, Serge entered the room. The thick-set, menacing, muscular guy pulled something out of his pocket: "Foot guy likes it a little different, so give me your right leg." He proceeded to remove the electronic GPS tag. Her leg felt strange, lighter and she gave her ankle a rub. Jada stuck her leg under the shower and washed it, over the week, the sweat and bodily fluids had left her ankle smelly and pale. She heard the door open and switched off the shower, grabbing a towel to wipe her leg. Turning she saw the 'foot man' enter the room with difficulty. He was wider than the doorframe, with neat hair and nice skin, just elephantine, with a bib belly and bloated cheeks that hung either side of his tiny wet mouth.

She walked slowly to the edge of the bed. "You're the foot man?"

"I am. My name is Francis, but ... people call me Franny," he said delicately to Jada's surprise. "Oh, you have such dainty feet!" The man wheezed and he held out his hand, beckoning her foot. She raised it slowly and he held it in his podgy hand whilst he slid his other hand around and down his enormous waistband, rippling down the fabric of his sweatpants.

He held her foot in his warm hand and whilst his hand worked away, he tried to tell her something, but she couldn't hear him; she was doing everything she could to zone out; she was looking through him, not at him. He pointed to the bed and edged closer to her. She felt her foot push into his belly and her leg crease and that did it for him. It was like controlled demolition, he went off; she ducked and he collapsed on top of her. It knocked the wind out of her lungs and her eyes bulged under the weight of the giant, sweating, unconscious man. Jada found her breath and looked left at the electronic tag that was on the small table next to the bed. This was her opportunity. She turned her head to the right and Franny's eyes were shut, his mouth was slightly open, tongue out, about an inch from her face. She turned away and he wheezed slowly, his warm breath on her neck started her wriggling in an attempt to get out and away. Jada could move her torso, but not her legs. There was nothing to grab a hold of to pull herself out of this fleshy mire. She gripped the sheets, trying to lift herself up, not quite able to get up on to her elbows, the fat man literally stuck to her. She tried again and again, but he was like a giant limpet and she slumped, arms flat on the bed, exasperated.

A moment later a voice behind her croaked, "Oh my God, are you okay?" Franny asked, his sausage-like fingers wiggling her shoulder. Jada exhaled and turned to him, getting a faint smell of peppermint.

"I'm okay," she said.

"How long was I out for?" he asked, and Jada

breathed in his sweet breath, evoking memories of her childhood.

"Just a minute or so," Jada said, her lungs still squashed under his weight.

"Okay, stand by, I'm getting up in three, two …" And with that Franny rolled himself over, away from Jada and got to his feet. He pulled up his sweatpants and held out his hand out to her.

"Same time next week?" Franny asked.

Jada didn't want to sound desperate or get a no, and she placed her leg in his hand and let her foot caress Franny's body from navel to sternum.

"Will you be ready to go, say … the day after tomorrow?" she said, and he squinted as his tongue wetted his top lip and he took a deep breath, looking down at her pretty foot.

"Definitely," he replied and a flicker of light in Jada's mind induced a broad smile.

"Day after tomorrow, then," she repeated.

*

Mal approached them unsteadily, the two plastic cups of hot chocolate in real jeopardy, the rocking motion of the ferry playing tricks with his balance. He stopped, mesmerised, resting on the gunnel and stared at Yazz. The golden hour rays wrapped a halo around her massive curls, which fluttered randomly in the strong, sea breeze. Yazz stood there, at the upper deck of the stern, looking out to sea, the golden light cutting around the clouds, glimmering diamond crests on the darkening waters. Little Al sat behind her, nodding off, bundled in a blanket on a deck chair, a disposable camera and personal stereo on his lap, the orange spongy headphones filling his ears with music. The crashing waves seemed to unsettle Mal's vision and his mind drifted …

    He saw himself hand-in-hand with Jackie, the ring he usually wore around his neck, as it used to be, adorning her finger. He remembered so many special dinners at Caesar's Palace on Renshaw Street, the ring clinking against her wine glass. He had her in that moment and now she was gone. They'd lost each other under the lights of every nightclub in the city. They had done it all and everywhere – the car, the beach, the pool – it had felt like the ecstasy would last for ever. Mal looked down, his mouth opened and cold spit dripped sideways out to sea. He felt nauseas, giddy, hearing Jackie's voice clear as day in his mind. She whispered, "I want us to try again, Mal." Her wet eyes spilling cold tears down his broad, muscular back, her gentle arms reaching around him, her hand on his heart as they laid in bed that Sunday morning. "I want us to be happy … start a family. We can do it. I love you," she said kissing his neck. It shut him down. He could not, would not tell her the truth. His personal ship had already set sail.

Mal blinked, back in front of Yazz. He handed her a cup of hot chocolate, which she sipped.

"This light is pure gorgeous, no?"

"Stunning," Mal replied, as he unclasped the chain from around his neck, sliding the ring off into his palm.

*

Aitch slotted Pop-Tarts into the toaster while *Baywatch* played on the large TV. He sat calculating what needed rewriting from the carnage of burned notebook pages that lay next to Blair's envelope of cash.

"Shit, I need to rewrite all this before I forget it," Aitch muttered. "Blair, got any paper, or a notepad?"

"Have a look next to Mal's trophies, mate," Blair directed, "through the blue door, first on the right."

Aitch made his way into the house through the blue door. The formal dining room, this calm space, had net curtains diffusing the light. Mal's bodybuilding trophies lined up on the long table, each one a peak of human performance and testament to his blinding and all-encompassing vanity. Next to them was a photo montage of a younger Mal, training and posing. Mal's sculpted arms, fed by bulging veins, wrapping his flesh like thick grotesque shoelaces. The artificially large body belied a truth that the smile could not hide, yet the smile was ever present, like it had an On button.

"Bloody hell, his arms look about to explode!" Aitch exclaimed.

The Pop-Tarts popped up. Blair brought one over to Aitch on a side plate. Aitch bit a corner and steam poured out, so he set down the nuclear-hot treat. Blair glanced up at the photos.

"Sign of the times. Frank had Mal all jacked up," he remarked, opening a drawer.

"Well, he certainly seemed popular," Aitch smiled, pointing to a picture of Mal between two women.

Blair handed Aitch a notepad and took a deep breath. "Mal dated Jackie, there," he pointed, "for years. Thought she was 'the one', but it never happened." He pointed to the other woman. "Then he met Linda, married her in six months and that was that."

Aitch examined the happy snapshots. "They all seem like good friends."

"Peas in a pod, those lot. Partying while I was fighting in Bosnia," Blair mused.

"Where are they now?" Aitch asked.

Blair shook his head. "Two years ago, Frank was banged up. I was working with Mal in

Amsterdam ..." He trailed off, exhaling deeply as he stared at Linda's smiling face. "Fuckin' hell. Saturday night, the girls drove back from the Haçienda in this bloody, tropical rainstorm. Fuckin' tailback on the motorway and then – BAM – fucking container lorry ploughs into the back of them. Tragic."

Aitch opened and closed his mouth mutely, struggling to swallow. "Shit," he said softly.

*

On the darkening deck of the ferry, Yazz held up the gleaming ring, eyeing it. "You never just found this!"

"Yep, pop it on," Mal urged.

Yazz shot him a dubious look. "Bit creepy. I've a better idea ..." She drew back her arm and hurled it into the black waves, "There, that's better. Off to Davy Jones' locker, or whatever."

Mal lunged forwards gripping the guard rail in panic, and his face fell. Dumbfounded he slowly turned back to Yazz. She held her face stoney for an extra moment, then broke into a smile as she opened her palm to reveal the ring, sliding it straight on her finger. "Fits perfect!" She grinned, leaning in to plant a quick kiss on Mal's cheek, his astonished look replaced in an instant with a wry, lopsided smile.

"Hey!" Little Al called. They both turned together and in a flash of light the lad snapped a picture of the happy couple with a disposable camera.

*

Back in Mal's kitchen, Aitch scribbled rapidly in his new notebook while Blair channel surfed. Having ditched his slashed fleece, Aitch sat in just a T-shirt, the envelope of cash now bulging in his trouser pocket.

"*Baywatch* and *Blind Date* – the perfect Saturday night duo!" Aitch declared.

Blair snorted, breaking down and cleaning his pistol on the table. "The *Blind Date* contestants are wet as shite." Blair sat forwards. "If I got picked, it'd be la-di-fuckin'-da; on my life, I'd do the full monty: exchange pleasantries, try the jet ski, eat the gratis meal … enjoy Benidorm. But at the end of the day I'm there for a reason. No messin', I'd bone 'er! Roger and out, thank you, Cilla."

Aitch laughed. "And on that romantic note, where's the loo?"

"Upstairs, mate. Follow your nose!"

He zipped himself up staring at his eyes in the oval mirror, exhaling, thinking … nothing came to him, the sound of the flush refilling the cistern drowning out his thoughts. Aitch paused outside the bathroom door, his shoulders twitched and he rubbed his bare arms. If he was going to be trapped in this mess, he had to stay warm and think this through. He could go back downstairs and try and get something out of contestant number one, but Aitch stopped himself, because either Blair was holding something back, or there was something else in one of these rooms he needed to find.

The adjacent bedroom door was ajar. He caught a glimpse of the made-up double bed and vanity table displaying a vase, 'a vase with a single fresh flower?' Aitch felt a little rush and crept into the bedroom. His eyes rapidly scanned the feminine trimmings – Silvikrin hairspray, Chanel No.5, and an ornate golden vanity set, hairbrush with an Egyptian goddess on it, together with a slim-handled, face mirror. Ruffling through the wardrobe he found women's clothes hanging, untouched. One set of drawers contained pristine, lacy underwear; the one below was empty. Aitch's thoughts raced. This wasn't a bedroom, but a carefully preserved tomb.

He slipped into the second bedroom where jeans, a boilersuit, smart black trousers and white shirt were strewn across the unmade double bed. Rifling through an open drawer he pulled out a massive sweater, then a slightly smaller one beneath. Under those lurked some magazines: *MuscleMag*, *Flex* and – Aitch's eyebrows shot up – a copy of *Fiesta*.

He got on his knees, fanned out the magazines on the floor and opened the dog-eared copy of *Flex*. A shiver ran through him. The article title read 'How Not to Cook Your Balls: An Overview of Anabolic Steroid Use.' Aitch scanned it quickly and stopped. Several passages were underlined neatly in red pen. A scrap of paper slid down the spine of the magazine. Aitch turned it over to see a red telephone number. Aitch's eye twitched as he shook out his toothpick container, slotting a quivering pick between his lips.

Blair's words echoed in his mind: "Frank trained Mal – got him jacked!"

Aitch's gaze fell on a disposable camera atop the bedside cabinet. Next to it sat a packet of photos held together with an elastic band. He thumbed through snapshots of the kid, in neat little outfits, playing in the park, and a bunch of a mud-spattered Little Al playing football. *What the fuck is going on with this guy?* Aitch thought.

"Al ... Yazz ... Mal," he muttered under his breath, sitting amidst the debris of centrefold flesh.

He shivered again and he looked at the smaller sweater. *It would have to do,* he thought, and grabbed it.

Aitch stuck his arm in the inside-out sweater, pulled and rotated his arm to get the sleeve in the right way and sat there looking at

Yazz's mobile phone number he'd written on his forearm. His eyes flicked to the bedside phone. He dialled Yazz's number.

"Hello?" said a male voice.

Yazz's number? Shit! He remembered this was Jack's phone, that Yazz had borrowed. Aitch stumbled along, immediately finding a voice "Hi, is Yazz there?" he tried in his best Glaswegian.

"No, who's this?"

Blair appeared in the doorway and Aitch waved him to stop and zipped his own lips quiet before continuing on the phone, "Ehhh, it's her brother, Graham. Is Yazz about, no?"

"Oh, hi. Yeah, she dropped my phone back about twelve-ish, I think. I was in the shower. She's not in now, though. I saw her leaving in a black BMW with some older guy and a young kid."

Aitch's eyes widened. "Okay."

"You want me to give her a message?"

"No, ta," Aitch hung up and breathed out slowly.

Blair took in the scene: the photos, the medical literature, the men's magazines.

"What the fuck's going on here, like?" Blair said.

"I've a bad feeling about this," Aitch replied slowly. "Mal's taken Yazz and Little Al to Amsterdam. And there's this number which marked this article in the magazine …"

Blair's expression curdled as the insinuation dawned on him. "Ring it, then."

Aitch did so, listened and hung up.

"Answerphone. Nordbatch Fertility Clinic."

Aitch turned to the wardrobe and opened a shoebox. "Letters," he said.

"Stop," Blair grabbed the box from Aitch. "This shit is private, you should keep your nose out of Mal's business."

Aitch let go of the box. "If you want me to help you find out who tried to whack your brother," Aitch waggled his head, stepping in closer to Blair, "we've got to check out this stuff. Do you really know what was going on with Mal when you were in the army?"

Blair didn't move a muscle. "This, this is the truth, in black and white. We can put it all back exactly how we found it," Aitch continued, "Mal doesn't need to know."

Blair tapped the pistol against his leg, thinking.

Aitch stood tall. "Don't you want to know if Mal's hiding something? I'm suspicious, you know and … scared, I don't mind telling ya."

Blair held out the box to Aitch. "I can't touch it, let alone read it, that's just not me."

Aitch blew in his hands and sat at the bedside table and began methodically opening the correspondence. "Letters from Jackie. Loads of them," he said, his eyes scanning the pages.

"Listen to this, from 1991: 'I'll always love you for getting me out of Amsterdam, but you can't just hold on to me. You've got to let me move on and have a family. I know you say you don't want kids, but I'm sure one day you'll feel different.'" Blair turned left and right, his right hand on his head, slowly breathing out, tapping the pistol on his left leg.

Aitch held up another letter. "This one is from the Nordbatch Fertility Clinic, 1993. 'Dear Mr Tanner, following treatments, examinations confirm your sperm count and quality mean chances of siring a child stand at less than 0.5 per cent.'"

Blair paced back and forth, assimilating this. He rubbed the barrel of his pistol to his temple in frustration before realising what he was doing and ejected the clip. "He can't have kids!"

Aitch met his gaze. "If Mal blames Frank for juicing him up on steroids and maybe making him infertile ... did *he* put Frank in the hospital?"

Blair punched the wall. "No! It can't be ..." he said and let his head fall against the wall. His arms rose up and levered himself off the wall as he turned back to Aitch, his eyes wide, "We've got to get to Amsterdam. Now!"

Downstairs in the kitchenette, Blair opened a set of drawers and pushed some items around. He picked out a screwdriver, a fountain pen and a yellow squeezy bottle of lemon juice, which he stuck in his jacket pocket. Blair marched down the corridors of inventory and stopped by the stack of car stereos holding up his hand to stop Aitch. Blair looked at the pile of stereos and then took a step back and scanned the warehouse. Aitch was way ahead of him, he picked up the stereo he had thrown at Pie. He hoped to fuck he hadn't broken it and gave it a little shake and nothing rattled, although he had to wipe some blood from the back off it on his sleeve. Aitch held up the stereo with a little whistle and a smile emerged from his partner in crime. Cold, fresh air hit Aitch as he stepped outside, their shoes slapping across the wet, concrete yard. He'd relax but was still shitting himself that the stereo might be broken. Blair pulled the sheet off of an old Renault 5 Extra; a small delivery van with two seats, they got in and he inserted the tape deck. Aitch gulped. The taillights illuminated, and with a cough of exhaust smoke the old van sprang back to life. The stereo however, was lifeless. The car idled as Blair gently revved the old girl, before looking at Aitch. "C'mon...tunes!"

Aitch held his breath, pressed a round button on the far left of the device and it illuminated and the cabin filled with pumping house music. The smart boy exhaled and the van sped off.

CHAPTER ELEVEN

The small farmhouse was just outside of Amsterdam, a village called Zuiderwoude. Upstairs in the immaculately clean main bedroom, the sterile smell of lemon-scented anti-bacterial cleaning products fought the air of tension and despair. Per lay sleeping in the bed, an IV drip slowly feeding fluids into his bandaged arm.

A few days of beard growth shadowed his pale, scratched face. His wife, Gem, sat with her back to the bed, phone pressed to her ear as she quietly delivered the grim prognosis.

"It's fifty-fifty whether Per will make it through the night," she said, her voice strained.

The tinny voice of Ville crackled over the line. "What about the other guy?"

Gem's jaw tightened, the business had changed her. "Only Alvar's order and my faith has stopped me from putting a bullet in that piece of shit," she said angrily; then calmly, "he's tied up in the pig shed." A slight pause, then Gem found herself back on the level, "How's my little nephew?"

The other end of the line was Rødbyhavn port, where Ville stood at a phone booth looking out over the ferry dock with his wiry-framed, taller but younger brother, Morten, figuring out how they were going to enact Alvar's plan. This was a complicated, family business. Ville tapped his brother to come closer, holding the phone out for him. "Not so little," Morten replied. The ferry's boarding buzzer went off as Morten stepped in. "Hey, Gem." Ville put the phone back to his ear. "Gotta go – see you in three hours." He replaced the handset back on the hook. The men turned and got back on their Harleys, the rear of their biker jackets displaying the Badbones insignia.

*

He'd come back tooled up, ready to teach that student twerp and Blair a lesson. As soon as he crept around the back of Mal's, he knew something was off; the back door wasn't locked and the Renault was gone. Whatever, he wasn't taking any chances, he'd already been humiliated enough today. The swallow on his neck began pulsating and he pulled out his Grandad's Webley Mk VI revolver and began clearing all the rooms. Five minutes later, confident he was alone he opened the cabinet in the glass-walled office and found a bottle of dark rum. "Fuck it!" he said, putting the revolver away and popped the cork. Three minutes later, the darkness had consumed him and he had his German trench dagger out, psyching himself up, slicing through every row of stacked boxes in the warehouse. In the living room he cut the soft blue curtains in half, slashed a Z in the antique oak table and stopped, eyeballing the row of shiny objects. A minute later, he swept his arm across the neat arrangement of trophies, sending them into a bin bag. Pie left the bag at the bottom of the stairs; he'd deal with those later.

Eric sat at his desk, lit by a lamp, writing. Under the spotlight his tiny Beretta 3032 pistol looked like another ornament. Resting his telephone under his chin, he read the number from an open notepad and dialled the square buttons with his good hand, his left arm still limp, laid on his lap. Eric put the phone between his chin and shoulder and picked up his Beretta, popping out the clip and looked closely at the bullet in the magazine.

Pie was sweeping the Egyptian brush and mirror set into his bag along with the nearly full bottle of Chanel No. 5 when his phone went off. Eric paused the caller for a second, listening at the top of the stairs – nothing – then started the call, walking into Mal's room. Eric wasn't one for small talk. He had paid Pie for answers.

"What can you tell me about Mal and Frank's expenditure and investments?" Eric asked.

"Mate, Mal's quite a character, always copping off with some bird and, um, I've heard, I know, he's got a bunch of kids, like, with some of 'em. He pays for everything, got them all set up so he can live a life of luxury whichever woman he's with," Pie blurted.

"I see, and what about his businesses?" Eric asked.

"He took over his ex-wife's salons after she passed and they just exist now to clean his money."

"Bank accounts?"

"Mate, I've seen his account, it never goes over twenty grand."

"My boss wants his hundred Gs back, or Mal is going to get a bullet."

"Mate, what can I say, the money is gone! Trust me, it's spent!"

There was a pause on the line as Eric placed the bullet back in the magazine.

"… and Frank."

Pie's trapped voice emanated from the telephone. "Frank's got nine grand in a children's saver's bank account, and five-and-a-half in what he seems to run his garage. That money has been in his account over four years, since he got banged up."

"Okay, thank you, Pie, that's very helpful.

Anything else I need to know?"

"Nah. Nothin 'you've got to worry about."

Pie ended the call and put his mobile in his pocket, staring at the clothes on the bed. Mal's trousers and shirt, thrown down, making a shape, like a fallen man. His eyes looked to the head of the bed, to something else. Pie kicked the small chest of drawers beside his bed where there was a framed photograph of Mal posing from his Mr England win in 1986, and it toppled over. With the clatter of the frame, he pulled out his member and hosed the bed with neon-yellow urine from the pillow across to the strewn clothes.

*

Blair drove the little blue van to the limit, the Prodigy's 'Charlie 'drum and bass mix playing at high volume. Aitch drank a bottle of Lucozade. Blair tapped his shoulder. Aitch passed him a can of Coke. Blair tapped the top. Aitch pulled the ring pull.

*

Jada sat in the café window, plotting her escape, looking out at the silhouettes that bustled past the neon signs surrounding Dam Square. Despite the debacle earlier with Franny, and Serge replacing the electronic tag, Jada could sense freedom was just an opportunity away. In her nine days she was paid two hundred guilder in dribs and drabs, pin money to get new underwear and make-up. Apart from this coffee, she'd only spent twelve, so she must get as much as possible before Franny's return visit. She put down her Americano, a red crescent of lipstick where she had slowly sipped away at the dark moon. She would have to be quick when the moment came; merciless and exacting. Jada checked her watch, she only had eight minutes left of her fifteen-minute break and hoped to hell that the cream, painkillers and whatever fizzy shit that was in the green pill Marjo had given her would kick in. It still hurt to sit on it, so she tried to look out and lose her mind to the good things in the city.

She had learned to switch off from bad shit as a kid. Her father had kept chickens, and whilst she loved them, it was her job to wring one of their necks and pluck one every Sunday.

Taxis and trams artfully wove between the constant flow of crowds, the bubbles of wide-eyed tourists marvelling at the spectacle of the city. She watched the workers clang steel barriers as they were offloaded and erected along the Rokin, the workers illuminated by flashes of orange safety light. The sponsorship banners and the main stage already constructed for tomorrows Run Zygo Marathon. The charity event had helped rehabilitate and rehome so many ill and disadvantaged children. *They were being saved*, Jada thought, she would have to save herself.

She looked at the big stage. Run Zygo. The city would be busy on Sunday ... more men pounding the street, might mean she'd catch a break. She checked her watch. Five minutes to finish up and walk one street away from all this hope and goodness, back down Warmoesstraat to the red-light district, its steady flow of punters, gawpers and rogues.

Jada sipped the last of her coffee and took a deep breath in and out, readying herself to leave her cocoon. Her cup hit the saucer as a loud thunderclap frightened her out of her skin. She wasn't sure, but she might have just lost control in that moment, now sitting on an extra wet sanitary towel, soaked in anti-septic cream *and* piss. Rain lashed the window of the café. As she sat back, the shadow of a looming figure fell across their table. Rainwater dripping from his coat, Mal glowered down at her with bloodshot eyes. The waitress bustled over obsequiously. "Good evening sir! Would you like a seat?"

"I'm fine sweetheart," Mal rumbled and looked past her to the moustachioed male shopkeeper, "I'll a take a quarter of your Moroccan Gold. And a couple of Diet Cokes." The shopkeeper nodded and went out the back to fetch the hash.

The rain came down in sheets. Inside Mal's

parked BMW, Little Al sat oblivious to the world, bobbing his head to his personal stereo in the back seat. Yazz turned from the lad as a muffled ringtone emanating from the front. She fumbled for Mal's mobile and answered, raising an eyebrow. "Halloo?"

A man's voice calmly demanded, "Where is Mal?"

Yazz bristled. "Ah, he's gone tae fetch us some hash. Who's this?"

"Tell Mal the meeting is tomorrow at 10 a.m., usual place."

"Naw, you listen here, mate," Yazz snapped, massaging her temples. "Hold on, too much info pal. Ma heid's pure spinnin'. Let me grab an ink stick tae write this shite down." She turned to Little Al softly. "Got yer felt tips, pal?"

Little Al looked anxious. "Where's Uncle Mal?" the child asked.

Eric's ear twitched. "Is that your little boy I can hear?"

"Get tae fuck!" Yazz snorted, her hand over the phone. "Me with some wee bairn? Naw, he's just Mal's mate's kid." She tapped her makeshift pen on the page impatiently. "Right, okay, go again – the time?"

"10 a.m."

"Got it."

"Usual place."

Yazz hesitated. "Oh … wait, shite, drawing a blank here. D'you spell usual with a Y, correct?"

*

The large projector flickered onto a fifteen-foot screen in Scheltema, Amsterdam's most prestigious bookshop.

A full crowd watched as the video presentation about the funding for a string of new children's homes built up in preparation for Amsterdam's most famous philanthropist to make the stage. Harry Van Zyl projecting the perfect image of himself into the crowd's eyes and minds. Harry shaking hands with dignitaries, laughing with others. Harry reading to an injured child in bed. Harry riding uphill through the rain on a charity bike ride. Harry in the flower market, running Amsterdam's most successful flower business. Harry smoking a cigar.

In the half-light, off stage, the real Harry shifted, his eyes closed, his thoughts drifting a moment, away from his PR reel he'd seen a thousand times. In his mind he heard the young girl cry out in pain. This was the life he had made for himself, a private room in the hospital he had raised over ten million guilders to build. It was past 2 a.m., and hearing the girl, he slipped out of bed and entered her room. She laid there with tubes coming out of her nose. "There, there sweetheart. Let me give you some more of the good stuff," he said, turning the dial of the machine that fed her pain relief. Harry smoothed her brow.

"Is that better?"

She half-opened her eyes to him and a faint smile appeared. Harry gently patted her thigh. "Can you feel that?" The girl closed her eyes and wiggled her head, no. In a low voice she whispered, "Thank you for looking after me."

"My pleasure," he replied as his hand slid up the sheets, tracing her feet and legs.

"Excuse me," the manager of the bookshop said as he tapped Harry's shoulder, "Mr Van Zyl?"

Harry looked up, "Meditating!" he blurted, raising his eyebrows. The manager smiled, impressed, "I'll intro you in a minute."

The manager took centrestage. "It is with great pleasure that Scheltema welcomes business guru, marathon runner, philanthropist, CEO of the Run Zygo charity, and author of ... *Zyllions*, ladies and gentlemen – Mr Harry Van Zyl."

Harry jogged out, grinning in a tracksuit, waved away the applause, and stood before a huge poster of his book. "Thank you, thank you all ... for coming out today. My charity work has been a driving force for change in so many children's lives over the years. Tomorrow, the fifth Run Zygo marathon aims to smash last year's record total of 3.3 million guilders, all of which goes to build children's hospitals and look after vulnerable children in the Run Zygo care homes across Europe. For those of you who are signed up to run – thank you. Let's do this ... together!"

The crowd burst into applause and whistled. Fans lined up to get their books signed while Harry settled behind a table, a little too low for comfort. The first man loomed over him, baring his yellowed teeth.

"I can't wait to learn how you *really* made your Zyllions," he leered. Harry maintained his camera-ready smile and signed the title page with a flourish. "The truth ... is right there," he said, tapping the page before shutting the cover firmly.

"Next!" called the manager.

*

In the Renault van, Blair and Aitch waited in the car park of Harwich ferry port whilst they waited, looking out at the harbour. Blair sat, sizing up the smart boy. Peter Gabriel's 'Sledgehammer' played on the radio as Blair fixed Aitch with a look. "So Yazz is just your pen-pal?" Blair snorted. "You know there's a difference between reading about something and *actually* doing it."

Aitch shifted, defensively. "I like writing letters. People write stuff they would never say."

Blair snorted again. "It won't get you laid,

though, will it?"

Aitch fizzed up. "You do know that *Blind Date* isn't real life."

Blair brushed Aitch off. "If you wanna play Mr Darcy, you'll end up with nowt!" he said, blowing out some air. "You'll either go mad or become a monk thinking like that." He cracked open another can of Coke. "When I shipped off to Belfast in '85 I was over the moon – beautiful fiancée, Nina, got a house deposit saved up, joint bank account. I'd never been more committed. Did it last? Did it fuck!"

Aitch looked quizzical. "What happened?"

Blair gazed at his drink. "I realised I was better off with cans than a big bottle!" Aitch looked perplexed as Blair continued. "Cans stay fizzy, bottles go flat," and with that, he lobbed the empty can out the window and belched.

"But … did you ever write her a letter when you were in Belfast?" Aitch asked.

"Fuck off, did I!"

Aitch raised his shoulders and looked down with a 'told you so' indifference.

"Letters don't mean shit!"

"I couldn't disagree more. Letters are worth every second you spend on them."

"Well, trust me, sometimes you just gotta cut off a piece of you if it's gonna cause damage," Blair continued, "that's just self-preservation, mate."

"Why would you not want to share your innermost thoughts with your fiancée?" Aitch said with surprise.

Blair's eye twitched. "Hey, who you are and what you do, *that's* what makes a man," he said. "Belfast changed me. I couldn't just lose my fighting spirit, I couldn't write about the shit I'd seen and done to Nina. She didn't need to know. You get me?"

"So, you sacrificed your relationship with Nina so you could continue being a soldier?"

"Well, that's ancient history, the woman I'm with now, I can come and go as I please, no promises ... no compromises."

Aitch blew air out the side of his mouth incredulously. "Hmm, maybe you should ask her how she's feeling sometime," he offered as he tapped his pack of Marlboro Lights and pulled one out. "Pass us those matches."

Blair got out the lemon juice bottle and the matches. Aitch lit a cigarette and burned his thumb, with a repressed cry he popped his thumb in his mouth. Blair got out the van and looked back into the big baby with a commiserating shake of his head.

"That's fate, maybe you should give up mate."

Blair walked to the back of the car turning

the lemon juice bottle over slowly, Aitch followed, popping his thumb out of his mouth. "What's the lemon juice for?"

Blair opened the back doors of the van and climbed in, "Mal's custom – throws off the dogs."

"Oh," Aitch replied, but still unsure of what that meant and turned back to the previous question. He took a drag of his ciggy, "I can't give up smoking, not hash anyway. Had a blast in Amsterdam last new year's. Met this weird lass in a coffee shop, offered to 'warm me up.'"

This pricked Blair's attention. "I knew you were hiding something. What was she? A prossy?"

"Maybe. I'm rolling a joint, her eyes are bugging out. I notice her lipstick is smeared across her nose, like she tried to do her lips on the bus, all the while she's nicking the sachets of sugar from my coffee. I light up the fatty and tell her my mate Jerome is next. She opens a packet of Drum in which she has some wet wipes, a letter and a pen. She tells me she's a rep for Mercedes and the letter is from her parents. They don't want anything to do with her. She starts scribbling on it, then rips up the letter."

"Psycho ... Did you shag her?"

"What the fuck? No! She had been disowned by her family, her own flesh and blood." Aitch sighed through pursed lips. "She stormed off. After that, my libido was like a wet book of matches." Aitch's cigarette burned down, leaving half a stick of ash.

"Fuck's sake, wet leg, should've let her have a toke and got yourself a freebie. You gotta change it up a bit, be a fucking man sometime."

Aitch was aghast, fuming, breathing hard. The ash dropped from the cigarette.

"What the fuck? I am a man, one with principles!"Aitch rubbed his head, turning around, "When was the last time you looked in the mirror?"

Blair stopped and looked up intensely at Aitch.

"Today." Blair stood away from the back of the van, still locked on to Aitch. "I spent my life fighting for other people, for all the wrong reasons, but this, this mission we're on, is the only compromise I'm willing to take. This is personal."

Blair stepped in to Aitch. "The question is, Mr Pen-pal, Mr-bleeding-Commitment, do you really think you'd be ready to fight for Yazz?"

"Yeah ... yes!" he replied as the idle cigarette burned his hand. "Ahh, freakin' napalm!"

Aitch chucked the fag down and stomped on it repeatedly and marched off in a huff around the corner of the van, jacked full of adrenaline, scanning the area.

CHAPTER TWELVE

The door opened to the large L-shaped room and Mal's hand flicked the light switch illuminating Harry's cavernous photography studio. "Power on!" Mal said, looking at the lad affectionately. The studio was pristine and white, photographic lights covered with white sheets with a mirrored wall to the left behind the kitchen area, in the middle of which stood a large wooden island and stools. Yazz and Little Al walked ahead of Mal, looking around the cool studio. The windows had shutters with white foamboard covers. The far-right hand side of the room was a lounge area, with a large sofa, table and a huge TV. The other side of the room from the front door were two bedrooms, one on either side of the white studio area. Mal set down a brown paper bag full of groceries on the wooden surface, lifted out a bottle of Sambuca and tossed a packet of bloody, fillet steaks on the island with a giant smack. The sound made Yazz and Little Al jump and turn to see the big man switch on his smile.

"Who's hungry?"

*

Aitch marched across the car park, seething. "Wet leg?" he said. "I'm a fuckin sledgehammer, you dickhead!" He stopped by a planter to pee, analysing his shadow. Leaning on the planter was a six-foot piece of scaffold. Aitch zipped up and grabbed the heavy steel. He lifted the pipe above his head, ready to catch his shadow unawares. He felt the darkness. "Die! You useless piece of shit!" he screamed, his whole body a demolition plunger, pulverising the steel into the concrete.

Blair waited, ears pricked at the first clang – then an animalistic cry followed by two more blows. Then silence.

A tsunami of adrenaline exploded from within Aitch as he dropped the pole. It left his hands vibrating, ears untuned. *This will pass,* he thought, trying to immediately calm himself. He turned his hands over and the skin was torn, blistered and bleeding.

Breathing hard, he thought he might pass out, and sat down by the bin next to the planter. On the ground Aitch's instincts kicked in, picking up a used takeaway box and a half-filled bottle of water. He washed his hands, tossed the chicken bones and unscrewed the partly used napkin to dry and compress his wounded hands. It would have to do.

*

9.37 p.m. Mal broke the safety seal on the Sambuca. Little Al and Yazz divebombed onto the huge couch and she punched the channel button on the TV controller: NPO1, No, NPO2 No, NPO 3 No, MTV, yes!

Mal necked his first shot. "Fire water!" he exclaimed, holding up his now empty glass. Hardcore hip-hop blasted out the speakers – Onyx 'Slam'. "I love this tune!" Yazz exclaimed. "Let's get the party started," Mal said, knocking back a second shot. Little Al and Yazz jumped up and busted some moves around Mal. "Come on, ya heathen, what have ya got?" she said, and Mal turned his back on her. Yazz span Mal back around, the old dog wearing a wry smile stood there bobbing his head, juggling four potatoes. Yazz met his eyes and felt some colour in her cheeks, "Cool!"

*

Sasha the cat sat on the garage roof outside the apartment block, staring across at the opened second-floor window, watching the silhouettes of the two men cooking; she knew the drill. Harry prepped the guinea fowl wearing latex gloves, carefully tracking macros in a journal, like a surgeon. He turned to Eric, standing, obscured in the darkness.

"I'll be running the children's 5K tomorrow before the main marathon. Is everything arranged for Mal's drop off?"

"Yes, but he's not with his usual crew," Eric replied from the shadows. "He's with some dizzy Scottish girl and a young kid."

Harry paused, a pairing knife and pat of butter half in the bird, "You know, despite going way back with Mal, I've always been wary of him." He moved closer to Eric, prayer hands in front of him. "He's a snake. The ledger doesn't lie and I've considered what your inside man has said." Harry let his hands down and symmetrically smooth on the kitchen worktop. He let his head fall down, then drew his hands and head back up to prayer position. "He's got to go. Have the Surinams dispose of him once he's made the drop."

Eric was surprised. Despite the past four years of carrying out some repugnant orders, the two of them had formed a special connection. They worked and ate together, sure, but Eric knew the other Harry too. Harry had the beguiling, outward persona people loved, the type people praised and would fund. His charity projects were breathtaking and his drive relentless. Eric took care of everything below board. Between him and the bookkeeper they processed kids, Kalashnikovs, drugs and dreams ... everything, *everything* got turned into money. Clean money. This, though, felt different. Personal.

Eric tilted his head, "What about the kid and the girl? Who will run the UK operation?"

Harry's right eye half closed, "Inform Mr Gibbs he will handle Mal's business. When Mal goes to the drop, you pick up Mal's companions. We can put the girl in the windows and the boy ... we can make another film with the new girl, Jada," he said a slow smile creeping across his face as he waved Eric off. "Go and arrange it. I'll finish the dinner," he said, pushing in the butter and pulling out the knife.

*

Little Al was curled up around a huge pillow, the nightlight stencilling the sleeping child in the darkness. Mal edged back slowly, closing the bedroom door, *ka-chunk*. Mal turned to Yazz, a smile spread across his face. She'd heard the door, so didn't bother to turn around, glued to MTV, she just poked her hand in the air to offer him the last inch of her joint. He gently scissored the joint between his chunky fingers, took a lug and slipped it back to her waiting digits. Pouring himself a large Sambuca from the now half-empty bottle, Yazz said, "The wee bairn off to sleep?" Mal took in a mouthful and let the liquorice tones float around his mouth, letting it down satisfyingly slowly, finding another gear. "He's knackered, he gets like that when we go on trips. Memorises the journeys. One day he'll be on fucking Mastermind and his specialist subject will be Road Atlases of Great Britain since 1994."

Yazz held out the now minuscule joint, "Well, it's nearly the end of the road for this joint, son, want a quick blow back?"

"If you're blowing and I'm getting it," Mal laughed.

"Serious, you cunt," she cut back.

Yazz blew the end of the joint and scooped the fire stick carefully from the ashtray.

She cupped her hands. Mal cupped his hands and got a decent blast.

He leaned back on the sofa with his hands behind his head.

"No bad at blowbacks, me, it's just a shame you didn't clean your teeth first ..."

"Cheek of it"

"... and wash your neck," Yazz added.

She pulled her legs up to stop Mal, who was now play-fighting with her.

"... when was the last time you changed your pants?" she laughed.

"I'm gonna get you," Mal said.

"When was the last time?" Yazz insisted.

"I don't … often," said Mal.

"Gross," Yazz blurted.

"I turn them inside out."

*

Mal had gone for a pee, and the break calmed everything down. They sat watching MTV on the couch, Mal swilling back-to-back Sambucas. Yazz had no idea how long for, somewhere between the last joint and the music videos, reality had blurred perfectly into a dream. Mal had fallen asleep too and she awoke next to the leviathan, his grey hair by her chest. She was trapped. She tried to lift his head. His hair was perfectly silver and intact, she slid her finger over a tuft, laying it back behind his ear. It was getting a bit cold and she couldn't reach the blanket on the edge of the sofa, so she jerked her body to wake him. He woke and she immediately felt nervous from his closeness. "Phew, you need to wash your hair, you bogan greaser, you'll have fleas in there soon you're no' careful. You itchy at all, no?"

Mal turned over to face Yazz. "What?" he said groggily as their eyes met.

Yazz froze. "Nothing," she said and quickly turned over, away from him.

CHAPTER THIRTEEN

The Badbones Harley-Davidsons charged down the N518 on the Gouwzee coast road, north east of Amsterdam. It was the last leg before the farmhouse at Zuiderwoude. Morten obsessively overtook his older brother. Something from childhood Morten would never drop: his impulsive nature. When they hunted elk it was the same too, Morten always had to take the first blood. It made up Ville's mind about how to carry out Alvar's plan, make it easier to exact. Ville had never cut anyone's head off. He would just tell his younger brother to stand back, as he would do the deed, then wait and let Morten's nature kick in. Ville let Morten overtake again. The kid brother challenged everything Ville did. Morten took the piss; his running joke, to debate the existence of Ville's childhood friend, who had, one day just mysteriously disappeared without trace. Morten relished every opportunity to reference Ville's 'imaginary friend'.

In the front room of the farmhouse in Zuiderwoude, Gem sat knitting by the front window, the pig shed across the yard to her left. She had to control her anger and focused her icy blue eyes on her creative efforts, poking wool up, turning the needles consistently. It was hypnotic and the only way she found she could hold everything together. This wasn't gonna be just a blanket, it was a course of therapy.

*

Five hundred guilder for a video, Serge told Jada. "Okay," she answered slowly. She was ready with a question, when Serge followed up. "You are to take the night off and be ready to perform tomorrow." Jada was desperate to rest so she could plan her escape. Maybe the universe had heard her call. Five hundred, plus her ball of guilders, could buy her a ticket out of here and a new start.

*

In the darkened bedroom, Little Al lay flat on his back, awake, eyes very much open. He popped on his glasses and peered out the window for a moment. It was cold. The bed was warmer and he climbed back underneath the quilt, his arm extending like a robot to replace his glasses on the nightstand.

*

Mal ran his hands through Yazz's curls, massaging her neck as she nestled near him. With his other hand he reached behind him to the low table to grab his final glass of Sambuca, snarling at the now empty bottle.

*

Harry and Eric were done, their two plates were clean, their knives and forks together. Harry pushed his plate away from him, "Tell me about the woman you have lined up for the video?"

*

Mal ran his hands through Yazz's hair, massaging the back of her head. "That's nice," she said softly, eyes still shut in a deep slumber. Mal kissed her neck and slid his hands down her back, peeling off her joggers like two giant mechanical scoops. Instantly, she recoiled in shock. "What! Get tae fuck Mal!" Yazz screeched.

In his bedroom next door, little Al was awoken by Yazz's screams. Reaching for his glasses in the dark, he knocked them to the ground. Squinting, Al got up and stumbled towards the commotion.

Mal tried to hold onto the shoulder of Yazz's T-shirt as she pulled away forcefully. It stretched and ripped. "I want you," Mal slurred longingly as he moved in. Yazz punched him with a venomous straight blast squarely on the nose. It exploded blood all down his T-shirt and sent him back, knocking into the low table. "Fuck off!" she hissed. Mal stumbled back into the kitchen area, his hands grasping on to the wooden island.

Yazz charged at Mal as if to kick him in the groin. Grabbing a fistful of her long dark hair, Mal whipped her around, swinging Yazz face first into the refrigerator door. She bounced off, stunned, her legs buckling. The back of her head smashed brutally into the wooden island before she collapsed limply to the floor. Spots of blood now flecked across the preparation area. Mal blinked in the half light, nursed his gushing nose, unsure of how much blood was pissing from it. Little Al toddled into the room, rubbing his eyes, "I lost my glasses" he said.

Turning quickly, Mal forced an awkward laugh, "Everything's okay, Al. I've just got a bit of a nosebleed. Go look for your glasses under your bed, sunshine," he suggested, pegging his nose, blood pouring on the floor. Al scampered off.

Behind Mal, Yazz rose up, grabbing a saucepan from the drainer, "Dirty, old…" she started as Mal turned. The pan flashed through the air, crunching sickeningly into the left side of Mal's face. Reaching instinctively towards the welt, Mal stumbled. Seizing the opening, Yazz swung the pan viciously again from the right, knocking Mal out cold... "Cunt!"

Standing over his crumbled body, Yazz hefted the pan up to her shoulder. "You could have fucking killed me!" she screamed, incensed. The rage left her as quickly as it came. Letting her arm go limp, she quietly replaced the pan on the stove with a metallic screech. Yazz stared down at Mal's massive, motionless form, watching his chest slowly rise and fall. *Phew!* she thought. Little Al came bounding back in, glasses now perched on his nose.

Instantly masking her fury, Yazz turned to him with a calm smile. "Uncle Mal's pure steamin'! Gonna sleep it off," she chuckled lightly. Approaching the confused boy, she lowered herself to his eye-line. "Don't worry sunshine, he's okay. Well, he's no dead anyway, but ... you don't look tired. I know, let's go for a midnight walk, eh?" Yazz proposed, eyes wide and nose wrinkled in feigned nonchalance.

"Go put on your wee jacket and trainers," she directed warmly. As Al hurried to his room, Yazz's smile vanished. Glancing up at the railway station-style clock, she saw it was five past midnight. "Fuck!" she whispered under her breath. Mal lay bruised and unconscious, a dark welt swelling on his left cheek. Grabbing a glass, Yazz held it under his nose, watching as it fogged with breath. As Mal stirred slightly with a pained groan, Yazz leaned down next to his ear. "You are a deluded man."

Yazz sprang up like a cat, moving with urgency. "Be quick, sunshine!" she called to Little Al. Grabbing Mal's black leather jacket, she slipped it on. It swamped her, she slipped it off. "You ready Al?" She called.

Yazz opened the door to Little Al's bedroom. He stood there with his jacket on but only one trainer, pushing his glasses up his nose. Diving to her knees, Yazz commando-rolled across the floor, scanning under the bed. Popping back up, she said, "Wait here a minute."

Peering around the door, Mal still lay unconscious. The clock read 12.08 a.m. Yazz raced to the front door, carefully retracing their steps while checking the couch, bags and floor for the missing trainer. Mal groaned and stirred. Freezing, Yazz slowly rose and crept towards him.

Mustering all her strength, she rolled Mal onto his side. Stuck to his lumbar was the Velcro strap of Little Al's shoe. Gently removing it, Yazz exhaled in relief. She secured the sneaker on the boy's foot. "Ready for a secret adventure?" she asked brightly.

As they turned to leave, Little Al grabbed the sleeve of her hoodie. "Shouldn't we leave a note?" he asked innocently. Crouching down, Yazz whispered "If we leave a note, it won't be a *secret* adventure." She winked playfully.

Little Al grabbed her extended hand. She looked down and noticed flecks of blood on her hand. "Just a sec," Yazz said and dashed to the bathroom. Catching her reflection, she steadied herself at the sink, adrenaline making her disoriented. She splashed the blood with water and rubbed her hands once on the handtowel. Done.

Her hand was already out to grasp Little Al's. "Let's go!" she said, and immediately stopped, put Mal's leather jacket back on and by the time they got to the door Mal's hands slapped the tiled floor as he struggled to rise. Pausing, Yazz reached up to the apartment's fuse box and flipped off the main power switch. Darkness, and they were gone.

*

The bikers turned right and almost immediately right again to the farmhouse. They passed the horse walker, stables and pig sheds adjacent to the main house, a female figure standing, backlit in the doorway.

Upstairs, Morten, Ville and Gem stood around Per's bed as the battered gangster tried to lift his head. "Don't get up," Gem said.

Per fell from two inches above his pillow, his face scratched and bruised, neck bandaged, surgical tape across his nose. Per's eyes connected with his brothers in arms. Ville put his hand down to grip Per's in solidarity. Ville looked at Morten. Morten brushed his lank, mousy hair out of his eyes and put his hands on his hips and breathed out slowly. "Where's the other guy?"

Gem turned to her tall nephew, "He's in the pig shed."

*

Yazz became extremely conscious of the little boy's tiny hand in hers. They were all alone in this big city and she wished she had just calmed the fuck down and enjoyed a night out with Aitch. She looked at the street signs. That wasn't going to help. Shite! She stared at the next road to cross, that's all she was going to do, put distance between them and Mal. Looking down at the wee boy, she squeezed his tiny, warm hand and gave him a smile as the rain gently pattered the street awnings. Yazz tried to walk with Al under the awnings to keep him dry. Heads down, darting across the roads, swiftly passing Marathon signage. Checking over her shoulder, Yazz spotted Mal trailing them from a distance. A car blared its horn, and Yazz realised she had stepped off the pavement into another road, and in an instant she yanked Little Al back as he stood in a deep puddle. "Shite!" she muttered under her breath.

They crossed the road and Yazz looked down

to her wee amigo. "Let's race!" she said with feigned enthusiasm.

*

The place stank of pig shit and Cain could barely see anything. A few lumens from the farmhouse outlined the beam holding up the tin roof and vaguely referenced the straw on the floor. He'd awoken face down on his exposed chest and managed to stay warm, his hands bound with rope behind him. Now he'd pulled himself back up and managed to spit out the last of the straw and muck from his goatee and mouth. He could feel behind him that he was tied to a grated pig trough. He felt the grate with his fingers to see if it might be rusty, see if he could use it to cut through the rope. His mind was racing, then he heard the farmhouse door and footsteps. Cain's eyes flicked up to the partially open shutter and he sat back on his knees. The door to the pig shed opened, and Morten stood silhouetted in the doorway. "Time to talk," he said. Morten stepped forwards, a metre in front of Cain. "Now!" he ordered. Cain did not move. Morten eyeballed Cain, counting back in his head three, two, one. He reached for his hunting knife at his hip and Cain launched like a missile at Morten, the top of his head smashing into Morten's chest, knocking him over awkwardly. Morten's knife fell on the floor next to Cain. Cain's eyes lit up.

CHAPTER FOURTEEN

Clutching Little Al's hand tightly, Yazz quickened their pace. Coming to Dam Square, she pulled Little Al behind a large, illuminated map as she caught her breath. Peering out cautiously, she watched Mal pass by, oblivious. Heart pounding, she inspected their surroundings, but everything was in Dutch, leaving her totally disorientated. "That was fun, eh?" she said out of the side of her mouth. Yazz turned and the boy was nowhere to be seen.

Her face went ghostly white and she bolted in sheer panic in the direction they had been walking … the same direction Mal had gone. Sprinting wildly up the street, Yazz scanned the interior of the bars and cafés but saw no sign of the boy. She raced back out, terror rising within her.

*

Cain laid on one side, desperately trying to use his bound legs to scoop back Morten's knife to his hands.

He breathed slowly, concentrating. This is it. The knife was behind him. His bound hands reached down through the mud and straw, his fingers like spider legs sensing for the cold steel blade. The door swung open again and a figure fixed a yellow lantern to the main beam. Cain's head flicked up, eyes wide open, trying to recognise the figure in the darkness. "Cain Pålsson?" Ville ventured.

Cain squinted quizzically and then looked down, away from Ville.

"Fuck off!" Morten exclaimed. "*The* Cain Pålsson?" he continued, turning to Ville, "your imaginary friend?"

Morten's hand whipped up and grabbed Cain by the throat, his pistol to Cain's nose, "Drop. My. Hunting knife," he said. Cain dropped the knife. Morten let go of Cain's neck and grabbed a rake from the tool rack and dragged the knife back over to him. Morten turned to Ville. "I always told you, your 'best 'friend was probably a piece of shit, bro!"

"Shut up!" Ville said, sticking to the plan, turning back towards Cain. "Who is trading our used weapons?" Cain was silent. Morten couldn't let it go, never could. "Wow, wow, wow, wait just a minute for the elephant in the room. Your disappearance has tortured my brother for years and—"

Cain stopped him, "You. You are brothers?"

Ville and Morten looked at each other incredulously.

"I'm asking the questions," Morten said.

Cain smiled, waggling his head in disbelief. "I don't see it."

Morten punched Cain in the face. Ville repeated, "Who is trading our weapons?"

"Fuck it, answer my brother before I get your blood on my hands," Morten added.

"If you co-operate, we'll spare you," Ville said.

"No we won't," Morten jumped in.

"We will," Ville stated.

"You want to know the truth, old friend?" Cain said to Ville.

"Come again?" Morten replied, head askew.

Cain sighed, "Truths hurt."

Morten and Ville looked at one another, both unsure of this guy. Ville's mouth went bone dry, old memories and childhood trauma all came flooding back.

"I'll talk. First, put down your gun. You can shoot me later." Cain said dryly.

*

Mal exited a café and continued to charge down the rain-slicked streets, like an uncaged gorilla, his eyes darting wildly around, his head thumping. He thought he caught glimpses of Yazz weaving through groups of people, and pursued her doggedly. Suddenly, near a café sign, she vanished from sight. Mal raced on, head down.

Distracted by voices, he ploughed straight into the side of a car pulling up to the curb. The female driver berated Mal angrily as he lifted his battered, bleeding face, panting heavily. Squealing in disgust, the woman sped off. He took a breath. Calmly he entered the club next to the café sign where he was sure Yazz had disappeared. Perhaps his eyes had betrayed him. No. He had a feeling about this place.

*

Cain turned to face Ville, his expression grave. "My father, Doctor Pålsson, treated your father after his accident. Right before he died, my father told me why we had to move so swiftly to Amsterdam."

Shifting his gaze to Morten, Cain continued solemnly. "It was his truth, but not the whole story. Sometimes it's only after a person is gone that you can gain new perspective … the whole truth."

Once more, Cain's eyes found Ville. "After losing his job in the accident, your mother couldn't afford your father's rehabilitation, his medicines, or care. While we played football in your garden, your mother accrued a 'debt 'as my father called it." A rueful smile crossed his lips. "She was a vivacious woman – so she traded old polaroids from her modelling days with my father as payment. It led to the only thing those situations ever lead to."

Morten tensed as Cain's focus returned to him. "You still want to shoot me?" A sardonic glint flickered in Cain's eyes. "Or I could help you find the gun trader who has double-crossed you … brother?"

Revulsion contorted Morten's features. "You are not my brother!" He said, looking Cain dead in the eye. Morten's hand moved towards his holstered pistol.

"Don't do it," Ville warned, voice edged with restraint.

But Morten ignored him, drawing his weapon and pistol-whipping Cain across the face. "You're a filthy liar!"

Spitting blood, Cain remained undeterred. "Really? Go to Cherry's in Amsterdam. Ask Cherry where to find Eric and Blair – they do the trading."

"They're just the soldiers," Ville pressed. "Who is their boss?"

A sly smile revealed Cain's bloodied teeth. "Nobody knows his name, or has seen his face. They just get orders."

Morten rounded on Ville, fury blazing.

"Bullshit. Let me finish him."

"You'll need me to ID your targets …" Cain wheezed out the words. "Once you find them, maybe they can lead you to their boss."

Jaw clenched, Morten flicked the safety on and shoved his pistol back into his waistband. "We'll make space for you in the back," he said.

*

Across the city, Blair pulled the Renault up to the apartment block, shifting into park with a measured exhale.

"This is it," he said, "This is where we stay, when we do the drop-offs."

"They're in there?" Aitch clutched the door handle.

"Wait," Blair said, "there's something I gotta tell you."

Aitch sat back slowly in his chair and turned to the driver.

"Last week, I got tangled up in an arms deal that went FUBAR'd. Now there's some people prowling around Amsterdam I'd rather not cross paths with again, ya get me?"

Aitch's eyes blew wide and started manically blinking, "Stop! Stop right there. I cannot believe you are only telling me this now. You can have your money back – I'm not doing this!" he yelped, twitching, shoving the cash-stuffed envelope at Blair.

"Look, nobody knows we're here, right? So, we'll just dart through the shadows like a couple of ninjas, find Al and Yazz and fuck off home, alright?"

"No. Fucking no," Aitch refused flatly. Blair smacked the envelope back into Aitch's chest.

"Time for action, smart boy!"

Aitch put his hands over his face. Blair grabbed him by the collar and started pumping Aitch into the seat, back and forth. Aitch hit Blair's hand off shouting at every pump, "Get. The. Fuck. Off. Me!"

Blair stopped, still holding him, he leaned in, "Or what?" he said.

"Or I'll kick your fucking teeth in?" Aitch spat, pushing away Blair's grasp, pointing at him like an angry statue.

Chuckling, Blair sat back casually. "That's the spirit! And you've stopped twitching." With a playful wink, he exited the Renault, flashing the pistol grip tucked into his waistband. Still shaken, Aitch stared in shock at the lemon juice bottle jammed in the front window. "Fucking hell!" he whispered.

*

Morten looked down at Cain's dirty, bloody face with cold detachment as he slammed shut the boot lid of Per's Saab. At the front door, Ville stood in a three-quarter-length, blue coat with corduroy collars and buckles and blue jeans, holding an open duffel bag. "That's better, you should blend right in," Gem said as she handed him a huge cleaver, which Ville wrapped in a tea towel. She then passed him a Beretta M9 pistol and two magazines. "Take the 20 clip too, if you get in a jam you'll appreciate a little extra," she said, handing him the long mag from a tote bag. "Thank you, for everything," Ville said. Gem held Ville's gaze. "Once he's identified the target, put a bullet in him from me," she said, without a blink. Ville nodded and gave her a hug, then turned to meet Morten's steely gaze. He threw him the keys.

"You got the address?" Ville's gruff voice sliced through the tension.

Morten caught the keys deftly. "Cherry's? A name like that, it can't be hard to find."

Ville stepped in close, his next words a hushed undertone meant only for his brother's ears. "Do you believe his story?"

Jaw tightening, Morten replied flatly: "He's lying for his life."

He turned and started walking towards the driver's side door. Ville followed, his whisper carrying an urgency. "But what if it's the truth?"

Morten whipped around to face him, putting half a dozen paces between them and the car. "The truth is upstairs. You've seen what he's done to Per. That guy in the boot is our sworn enemy."

Ville held his ground, increasing the distance. "But he might be of our blood."

The words hung heavy in the air. Finally, Morten spat out two words with contempt: "Bad blood."

Ville was caught in the moment, unsure. Morten hit Ville's left shoulder, "Let's go to work."

Without waiting for a response, Morten slid into the driver's seat and slammed the door shut, sealing them off from any further argument for now. "What are you wearing?" Morten asked.

"We need to remain low-key," Vile said. "I got you a change of clothes in the duffel bag."

"I'm not changing," Morten said, accelerating away. Driving the Saab was a million miles away from the Harleys: a clean, sterile, rocket ship that seemed to float over the tarmac at light speed towards their grim destiny.

CHAPTER FIFTEEN

The apartment door was slightly ajar, only the edges of the expansive studio illuminated in the moonlight. Blair halted Aitch silently outside. He slipped in, taking careful steps, sweeping the space, both hands on the pistol.

Aitch stood in the silence, contemplating exactly what he could do if this all went tits up. *Bloody hell*, he thought, this was taking too long. His heart began to race, so he took in a deep breath, ready for action.

Aitch listened to cupboards closing and the rustle of clothing.

"Clear!" Blair called and Aitch let out his breath. Blair came back to the front door and flicked on the main breaker switch. They entered the apartment with the lights on and the blood splatters leapt out at Blair, "Shit a brick! Check out the claret on the fridge door and the side of this table!" Blair noticed he had blood on his finger tips and he wiped them on his bandaged right hand.

"Fucks sake!"

Aitch looked at the blood on the fridge, his jaw dropped and he turned and looked out the window. Aitch turned back holding up his hand, "Stop, wait! I have an idea of where Yazz might be!"

"Where?" Blair asked.

Aitch had a moment of calm before they walked into the Wave Bar. He'd told Yazz all about it, describing the hot pink Cadillac sofa and the chill vibe the place had. The doors opened and they entered too quickly to be diners. Aitch and Blair's eyes swept the crowded tables and secluded booths. Couples looked up. An old man and a younger man flashed them a questioning look. Aitch turned away from their penetrating gazes. "Dammit! I really thought we'd find her here, I'd written to her about this place," Aitch admitted, pacing anxiously. Blair stopped him gently with the back of his hand. He looked out at the city lights through the window for a moment, calculating. He gestured to Aitch's untied laces and said calmly, "You know what I think about letters. Now, tie your shoes and get ready to run."

Blair wasn't kidding, they tore off down the rain-soaked streets once more, past men in rain coats and couples huddled under brollies escaping the messy drizzle. Blair ran with Aitch, giving the young lad sound-bite prompts to which Aitch could only reply in grunts and nods. *Chaka, chaka,*

chaka went Aitch's percussion. All the knowledge wasn't enough and the kid stopped under an awning with heaving gasps. "I thought you said this place was close!"

"Come on!" Blair blasted, rain dripping from his face. Aitch rubbed his soaking hair and squeezed out his drenched sleeves. "Wait! Just ... stop," Aitch said. "This is madness – where are we going?"

Blair grabbed Aitch's sleeve, yanking him back into the downpour. "Cherry is *our* contact for *all* our business in Amsterdam. She's our best shot at finding Yazz and the kid."

"What happened to being a couple of ninjas?" Aitch replied exasperated.

"You saw the blood in the apartment." Aitch's eyes opened wider and he drew a slow breath. "Time to go on the offensive!" Blair continued, and patted the kid's shoulder enthusiastically.

They ran some more, Aitch looking down and up continuously, being careful not to splash himself or slip. Aitch was getting disorientated and nauseous. The darkness and neon reflections in the puddles enveloping him, filling the kid with a sense of dread. He felt like a maggot eating through a rotten fruit. They rounded what was the final corner, and then they stopped under the glowing sign, 'Cherry's', the name underscored by a neon outline of a pair of glowing cherries on a stork. Aitch shook his head in dismay, "You have got to be fucking kidding me!"

The freezing rain continued to pelt down as Blair assured Aitch, "This isn't just the best whorehouse in Amsterdam, it's the eyes and ears of the street."

Still hesitating, Aitch retorted, "Give me one good reason why I should go in there." Blair tapped the envelope bulging from Aitch's pocket. "You got five thousand, four hundred and fifty reasons in your pocket." Aitch swallowed hard. "Plus, I've been banging the madame for a couple of weeks – off the books. If anyone knows what's going on, Cherry will." Blair added.

"Cherry's … your girlfriend?" Aitch asked incredulously.

A security camera greeted them as they entered the lurid, hot red lobby. A bored desk girl popped her gum. "Good evening, do you have a reservation?" she droned in monotone.

"I need to see Cherry. Now," Blair demanded in a glacial tone, water dripping off him. The girl glanced up.

"She's unavailable. Would you like to see our services instead?" she said pointing to a menu on the counter. As Blair loomed closer, his manner intensified, she recoiled slightly.

"No thanks, just buzz Cherry … now," he ordered through gritted teeth.

Flicking her eyes towards the security cameras, she replied nervously, "I can't do that, if you don't have an appointment …" In one quick motion, Blair slipped his pistol under the counter, an inch from her groin.

She looked at him terrified. "Buzz that door open right now, or I'll fill your hole full of lead," he whispered menacingly. Trembling, she hit the buzzer. Blair poked her abdomen with the pistol, "Call for help-and the next bullet is for you."

The walls of the dimly lit corridor were lined with carpet, suppressing the sounds of moans, whips and pounding music. They turned a corner and a pair of crumpled legs spilled from a doorway; Blair held his pistol out ready and signalled Aitch to stay behind him. They moved in carefully, the floored security guy had a bullet wound to the chest. Blair crouched down low and swung into the room fast, extending the pistol, sweeping the upturned room. Clothes, shoes, make-up, sex toys all shaken up about the place. In the middle of the room was Cherry, bound to a chair, duct tape over her mouth, mascara trailing down her bruised cheeks. She squinted as she saw a different Blair, looking away in abject horror. Replacing his gun in his waistband, Blair hurried over to peel the tape off. Cherry froze, terrified at his touch. "Hey, hey, it's me, Blair," he said. Cherry had no breath; two tiny exhales and he shook her shoulders gently. She took in a panic breath, like a free diver reaching the surface, and finally her eyes met his again, staying wide open, letting him back in. "I thought you were dead!" she softly cried, and held him at arm's length a few more seconds.

"Nah. Who did this to you?" he replied calmly.

Cherry's black tears ran faster and she tried to bring Blair closer, but buckled in agony, coughed up blood and clutched her stomach.

"Badbones guys, they ... they wanted to know about the boss, everything about him."

"What did you tell them?"

"As little as possible!" she exhaled painfully, in a weak voice. "I couldn't take the beating any more, so ..." She held up her hand, pausing as she drew a slow breath, her other hand on her ribs, "so, I— I gave them Jada's address."

"Who is Jada?"

Cherry took several short breaths. "She's the new video girl ... Probably getting wasted, cos Eric just picked up a little boy for ... tomorrow's video shoot." Cherry grimaced. "She hates doing that paedo crap."

Blair's eyes blew wide with alarm. Helping Cherry to the sofa, he asked intensely, "What? What little boy? *What* little boy?" he said giving her a little shake.

"I had to give them something, or I'd be

dead," she said, her eyes wide. "I have to warn Jada."

"Forget Jada! *What* boy? Cherry, I wouldn't even be here but my little nephew has gone missing with Mal."

Aitch stood forwards, "And my girlfriend, Yazz."

Blair sat Cherry back down and turned away. "Oh my fucking Lord!" Blair said holding his head in his hands, "this changes everything." Blair breathed out turning a full three-sixty. "I'm gonna need Eric's address. Come on, come on!" Cherry's head was tilted, her panda eyes a big wet mess as she scribbled Eric's address.

"Oh my God, I'm sorry, I ..." she managed with a pained grimace. Blair got down to look at her and took the address. "Thank you. Listen, you're gonna be okay," he whispered to her.

Blair began to pull away from Cherry and she fell to her knees, exhausted and weeping, her arms wrapped around his legs, "No ... I'm not," she said, looking up at him, "Take me ..." Her words trailed off, "... sex, the sex," she seemed to whisper. Blair looked at Aitch, to the female bear trap around his ankles and back to Aitch.

Blair cleared his throat and pulled her back up gently, then leaned in, kissing her softly on the lips. "I can't take you with me, not now," he said, and as he attempted to pull away from her she passed out and slid to the floor, her hand open with a small bunch of keys in it attached to a Citroën key fob.

Aitch stuck his head by the doorframe, listing to hear. He whipped around to Blair and Cherry, "Someone's coming!"

"Here," he replied and threw Cherry's keys to Aitch, lifting her lifeless body over his shoulder, "go, go, go!"

He ran as carefully as he could down the hallway towards the emergency exit, kicking the metal bar with his boots. The back of the brothel had a small lamp outside, which shocked Aitch's eyes, like leaving the cinema mid-afternoon except he was in the middle of his own drama. The light reflected against the rain, it made Aitch blink to focus on the cars parked opposite, their five nose badges gently illuminated. Aitch saw the Citroën CX, and not looking down, made a beeline for it. He didn't see the broken tarmac and splashed through the puddles to unlock the door and held it for Blair to lay Cherry on the back seat. Blair stood his ground. "Get in, help me from inside," he commanded, totally pumped. Aitch slipped inside and held her head as Blair swung her legs in. Blair got in to drive and Aitch tossed him the keys. The car rose up on its hydropneumatic suspension, and after negotiating the deep holes in the car park sped away like a hovercraft.

Blair turned on the windscreen wipers and spoke over his shoulders, "Check her pulse."

Cherry's face was cut and bruised. Aitch felt her wrist. Nothing. He told himself not to worry and moved his fingers. Blair was reading the address and taking corners late. Aitch slid up to the side window.

"Sorry," Blair said, then looked up to the rear-view mirror. "Come on, talk to me kid, have you found her pulse?"

"No," he replied. "I— I can't feel a thing. Fuckin' hell, I don't know what else to do!"

"Right, get on your fucking knees, in the well," Blair instructed, "pinch her nose, and give her mouth to fucking mouth."

Aitch's heart was racing, this was unknown territory, he had no idea what was going to happen. He just knew he didn't want this woman to die. He did what he was told and slipped into the footwell, his right elbow resting on the seat. This was closer than he ever expected to be to this woman, right in her personal space. He saw her smudged lipstick and broken, bleary cobwebs of mascara around her eyes.

"Do it!" Blair commanded, "just do it!"

Aitch took a deep breath, pinched her nose and felt himself wince as his lips covered hers and he breathed into her mouth. He came up just as Blair jammed on the brakes at a red light, throwing Aitch into the back of the passenger seat, knocking the air out of him.

"Sorry!" Blair blurted.

Aitch fell back and held on to the passenger seat and caught the eye of an old guy waiting to cross the road who just stared back. Aitch composed himself and with another huge breath he inflated her lungs. Suddenly the car launched away and Aitch face-planted the back seat. He sat up and looked at Cherry. His mind and body seemed detached as he tried to cognitively process what he was seeing. He realised he could barely hear anything, trapped in his head with just his heartbeat booming away. Jacked full of adrenaline, Aitch slid his shaking hands and arms between the giant, ragdoll of a woman and the seat and tried to lift her up, but her head arched precariously back. Blair glanced around, "Keep going, son!" he shouted.

"It's not working! Nothing's working!"

Blair slammed on the brakes and skidded to the pavement. He turned in his seat and grabbed Cherry. She was held up by Aitch who had completely fallen to the back seat, his arms weakening from holding her dead mass. Suddenly her weight was gone and Aitch fell back, gasping.

Blair shook Cherry violently. "Come on, you fucking bitch! You're not gonna to fucking die on me!" Blair shouted as he continued to strike up a fresh spark of life, but she was gone and her head just hung back lifelessly.

"Stop, Blair! Stop! Just let me try again,"

Aitch shouted and he took her weight and laid her back down. Aitch put his face down and spoke into her ear, "Breathe ... come on!"

"Try mouth-to-mouth again!" Blair said as he put the car in gear.

"I am, I am, just drive will ya!" Aitch replied.

Blair looked at his watch, then pulled away again into the traffic.

"Now!" Blair snapped.

Aitch composed himself, took a deep breath and locked his mouth onto hers. He felt the pressure of his breath enter her lungs. He withdrew and looked at her face for any sign. Nothing. He placed his trembling hands in a triangle over her heart and pressed; one, two, three and kept going for another cycle. He finally stopped, took a breath and then blew into her mouth again. He held her face, gently, fingers to her right cheek, his thumb under her chin. He inhaled furiously through his nose, psyching himself up. "This is not it!" Aitch said and got down, nose to nose and screamed at her, "Cherry!" As he lifted his head back up he brought his right hand down and slapped her, hard. Tears came to his eyes, "No, no, no!" he shouted and he smacked her again and again with real venom. The final time her head flipped to profile, knocking her mouth open. The slap resonated so loud, Blair looked back. Aitch looked at her mouth, her teeth and lips for any subtle movement and the moment shattered as she let out a series of coughs and groaned as she swung herself upright. Aitch flopped down, next to her on the back seat, shaking and laughing like a maniac for a few seconds. After a few sobering breaths, he put his arm around Cherry, pulling her into him a little, resting his sweaty brow on her shoulder. Aitch looked up and saw Blair's eyes in the rear-view mirror, they were wet and shone as the soldier bobbed his head. "Fuck me, that was emotional!" Blair said, his voice trembling. "You did it, you little shit!" he said wiping his sleeve across his face.

Blair looked at Aitch in the rear-view mirror. Cherry's body bumped forwards like an unhinged box car, her head next to his, chin resting on the seat as Blair turned to kiss her forehead.

CHAPTER SIXTEEN

Damn, meat could be so annoying. Eric looked at the nails on his left hand and pushed his forefinger up against his molars, picking at the pulpy fibre stuck between his teeth. Periodically he swiped his tongue to relocate the offending scrap. Opening the car's glove box, he moved aside his small Beretta pistol and pushed around through the contents looking for something to poke the offending meat with. The little motherfucker.

*

Mal entered the packed, tropical-themed nightclub and brushed the cold rain off his head. He thought the shower had put out his emotional fire and he stood there doing his best to examine the veritable ants' nest of humanity before him. He was desperate to find Little Al and Yazz, but didn't want to attract attention, so took a slow pan of the location, letting his eyes hunt for the details of his prey. The place was a paradise of palm trees, banana plants and raffia work screens, all of which proved a nightmare for Mal as they seemed to obscure the critical features of everyone in the joint. After what seemed like a few minutes, between the hustle at the bar and dancefloor, Mal's vision was a swirling miasma, milliseconds of eyes and teeth and hair.

Mal tried desperately to focus as a tall, skinny dealer with mid-length mousy hair and a rat-like face sidled up to him somewhat too eagerly. "You need some blow, my man? Good price, good shit," he offered. Mal had his own proposal. He picked the scrawny fella up by his belt and swept him in an arc, sticking him behind a large banana plant. "I'll tell you what. I want five hundred guilders for the twenty premium disco biscuits I've got in *my* pocket. Fucking A-grade – all-nighters," he said, showing Ratface a small clear bag of white pills. "You're a crazy son of a bitch," Ratface snorted, noting Mal's dead stare. Ratface refocused his eyes on Mal. "Alright, gimme the pills."

"Show me the money. Pull out some bills, count 'em here so I can see," Mal countered, pointing to a table and stool camouflaged by the fingers of a large Swiss cheese plant.

Ratface sat on the stool and counted out the cash, but instead of paying attention, Mal got distracted, catching sight of Yazz at the bar.

Mal didn't look back, he just reached behind him, grabbed the money and ploughed through the revellers. Ratface stumbled off the stool and the gap in the revellers closed. The noise of the club drowned out his shouts and Ratface narrowed his eyes. He pulled out a knife from within the lining of his coat and forced himself through the sea of partygoers.

Mal spun the girl around by the shoulder revealing a stranger's face, just as the incensed Ratface caught up. She recoiled, her bare arms flailing, knocking over her boyfriend's whiskey down the back of a small Asian guy in a smart white shirt. The now whiskey-soaked Asian guy spun around angrily, slamming his shoulder straight into Ratface's stomach who reflexively slashed out with his blade, catching the girl's bare arms. Blood flicked across Mal's face. The girl's resulting shriek set off a powder keg of violence. As blood spurted from her gashed arm, her boyfriend lunged at Ratface. The whiskey-soaked man brought his fists up and let off a fierce Muay Thai kick, pivoting off his front foot, sweeping his leg up and over, smashing through Mal like a tsunami, buckling his arms and sending a shower of notes high above the partygoers. Through the hypnotic rain of notes, an arm extended firing a lethal cloud of mace into Mal's eyes. The big man felt a boot in the back of his knee, knocking him into several revellers and pulling them all down like angry dominos. Mal's head splashed down into the blood-and-alcohol-soaked floor. He lifted his cheek up from the sticky carpet, trying to open his eyes, which stung like hell. Mal brought his arm up, grunting, feeling about for something to grab, totally disorientated; a small hand grabbed his and pulled Mal up, just enough to lever another Thai kick. The boot struck Mal's temple, instantly knocking him out.

*

They had parked the Citroën across the street from Eric's. Blair had found an Evian bottle in the door compartment and Cherry's .38 snub nose in the glove box. He gave her both, she took a sip of water and sat curled upright in a foetal position, her face hidden by her knees. Aitch sat with his face pressed against the rear window, a huge space between him and Cherry. It was dark and the passing cars were all headlights and blurred blobs of colour as they sped by, spitting up fresh rain. Aitch was on tenterhooks waiting for a moment to exit the vehicle, his hand on the door handle. "Back in a jiffy," Blair said to Cherry, who gave a tiny nod.

Blair licked his dry lips. "You gonna be okay?" he asked.

Cherry lifted the .38 and cocked it. Suddenly, there was a space and the door handle clunked and Aitch was gone in a flash. As he shut the door a car passed an inch too close, catching Aitch, twirling him like a top. He span out of control and as he fell face down, the toothpicks from his top pocket shot out and surrounded his body as it slapped on to the wet road. The car screeched to a stop.

Fuming and miraculously in one piece, Aitch peeled himself up off the tarmac and shook his head, eyeing the illuminated brake lights on the back of the car. He charged towards the vehicle screaming, "You fucking moron! You coulda fucking killed me!" then smacked the quarter panel angrily. Eric climbed out, eyeballing his accuser. Blair rushed up behind Aitch clapping him supportively on the back, "You alright, kid?"

Eric's eyes opened wider,"Blair?!"

"Fuck it!" Blair growled with the last of his breath and sprung past the kid, leaping to tackle the driver. Eric was already leaning back into the car, scrambling for the pistol tucked in the glove box. Blair wrenched him backwards, sending the Beretta clattering in the footwell. Eric hung on and tried to mule-kick Blair, but the fiery, ex-soldier had a firm grip of the driver's left leg. Blair didn't let go and Eric's nails scratched across the driver's seat as the connected combatants crashed out of the car. Eric's head slid off the driver's seat, thwacked the dirty door sill and cracked on the concrete.

Eric's momentary airtime unsettled Blair's balance and he quickly stepped back, tripping over a dislodged curb stone. Seeing his opening, Eric flipped over and raced to the now-floored Blair, kicking him wildly. Swinging his leg back for a second strike, Aitch came flying in, toppling Eric off his one leg and into a small grassy area.

"Nice one, kid!" Blair croaked, half up already. Blair launched himself at Eric, who was face down on the grass. He punched Eric in the back of the head.

Aitch stood back, as Blair continued scrapping.

Eric turned over quickly and whipped an elbow into Blair's jaw, knocking him off for a count. Eric scrambled to his feet and kicked the disorientated Blair in the gut. Aitch grabbed Eric's shoulder, "Oi" he shouted. Eric turned, blasting his fist into to Aitch's face, and he dropped. Eric jumped on Blair's stomach, kneeling on his arms, smashing Blair's face. "You shoulda stayed dead!" he jeered. Blair could barely breathe, his head was spinning, he tried to move his face away from the strikes. *FUUUCK!* He was pinned. Blair summoned everything he had to wriggle and bounce his body to make space between him and his assailant. "Fuck," his ground game was weak. "Come on," Blair shouted at himself, this wasn't going to be the way it ended. He'd been in some fucking hairy situations in battle and this douchebag wasn't going to get the better of him. Blair used his legs to power off the floor, lifting his pelvis, when he heard a whistle. Eric was already slightly off balance and turned at the signal. The broken curb stone struck Eric just under his eye socket with a *SKLUTCH* and dropped him in the dirt. This time there was no dialogue, the smart boy was on fire, panting hard with rage.

*

Everything was still a blur. Mal pleaded blindly with the security staff. "You gotta let me go! I lost me son out there! Just tryna find our kid," he tried desperately. The pulsing music drowned out his appeals and he felt strong hands clasping his wrists and he let himself be led out of a door to a hit of oxygen and swirling blue lights.

*

Eric's eyes reopened in his kitchenette, which jutted out, separating the large main room from the front door. The bloody rag was so deep in his mouth he couldn't get enough air into his lungs. Zip ties bound his wrists to the wooden arms of his dining chair. He sat absolutely still, Blair holding the tip of his kitchen knife steady under his chin, watching his adversary's eyes refocus. Without warning, Blair flicked the blade up a few millimetres from Eric's eyeball.

"You are this close, you got it?" Blair said. "Just answer the questions or this is gonna get messy," he continued in a low voice. As Eric recoiled involuntarily against his restraints, Blair barked "Hold still ..." Before Eric could react, Blair began stabbing down between Eric's splayed fingers building up speed. "... I'd hurry up, I'm pretty rusty at this!" Blair continued, but Eric looked right through him.

"What have you done with Mal, the girl and little boy he was with?" Blair said, and threw in a slap which got Eric's eyes back on him. Blair sped up his stabbing, nicking Eric's fingers. Eric let out a muffled scream, nodding at Blair, who paused his assault.

Removing the saliva-soaked gag, Aitch waited expectantly for Eric's response. "I don't know who you are talking about," Eric wheezed breathlessly.

Blair leaned in close, resuming his staccato stabbing rhythm.

"Really?" Blair said. "See, that apartment downtown is a real bloody mess," he said holding up his bandaged left hand.

Eric took a short breath, his eyes shifted to Aitch. Blair left the knife quivering between his trembling fingers. Eric paused before exhaling, at which point Blair swiped the knife up across Eric's cheek, sending blood across the kitchen cabinets. Eric screamed in pain, arms tensing.

"Who was sent to do the hit? Where are they?"

Eric panted as blood trickled off of his cheek on to Blair's bandaged hand.

"Where are they?" Blair repeated, leaning in.

Eric waggled his head. "The hit is tomorrow at ten … after the drop-off. Just Mal."

"What about the video?"

"What video?"

Blair slowly sliced down into Eric's pinky, and he agonisingly grunted, eyes bulging.

"With Jada. We know about that," Blair said.

Eric's pinky bled profusely and he tried to breathe slower and deeper. The oxygen gave Eric a euphoric high.

"Okay, okay. I was ordered to grab the little boy for a video."

"What about the girl? What's he want with her?" Aitch added.

Eric turned from the knife to face Aitch. Aitch switched an angle poise lamp on, blinding Eric.

"I don't know, and I don't care. Why don't you two go fuck yourselves!"

Both men reacted instinctively, their fists crunching into Eric's mouth simultaneously.

Eric looked up, his battered face shining with sweat and oozing blood.

"Go on. Do it. Kill me," he said slowly.

Blair moved in, the knife parallel to Eric's

left eye. He could do this, like he had done many times before and would not lose a seconds sleep.

Eric blinked in the silence.

"Nope. Tape!" Blair ordered.

Aitch threw the gaffer tape to Blair, who stuffed the rag back in and taped it in place. Eric moaning, his eyes bulging. Blair opened a few drawers and cupboards, grabbing a box of 'All Night' sleeping pills and the glass lid of a wok. Blair hit Eric on the head with the wok lid, then ripped out the gaffer tape and rag. Eric took a huge panic breath and Blair slapped the sleeping pills into Eric's mouth, pinching his nose.

"Swallow!" Blair re-gaffered Eric's mouth and momentarily stood behind the seated man and squirted super glue onto the glass wok lid. Blair opened Eric's right hand and stuck the awkwardly large, glass lid to it. "Now you ain't grabbing anyone, you fucker!" he said, and turned to Aitch, "oh Vienna!"

CHAPTER SEVENTEEN

It was just after midnight and time for the leggy Kiwi and her half-cut Irishman to make a decision. The twenty somethings had been on a European adventure and according to Rowanne's watch if they got into this hostel now she could bag seven hours' kip before the 8.30 a.m. call time for tomorrow's marathon. The beers in Amsterdam may have been small, but there was no time for the muscular half-back to have just 'another one'. She swung around to stop Darren passing the backpackers' hostel, her running shoes tied to her enormous backpack nearly kicking him in the face. "Jeez, Rowe!" Darren said as he bobbed out the way, Rowanne's eyes instantly catching Little Al, all alone, staring in the window of the café next door. A small child out on the streets of Amsterdam after midnight? It was just instinct – she got down to make sure the kid was alright, "Hey there, little guy, where's your mum and dad?" Little Al turned and Yazz ran from across the street at full pelt, Mal's leather jacket flapping behind her. Car horns blared and she sped up, jumped on the pavement as a car shot past and couldn't stop herself, running straight into the café window. Yazz bounced off the glass, shaken and absolutely breathless, turned dizzily to Rowanne, "What ... What ...What are you doing?" she managed, bending over, swamped in the huge, black jacket.

"Well, I was going to ask you the same question, this little chap'll catch hypothermia unless he gets in the warm," Rowe said. Yazz, was still bent in half, lungs burning. Darren got down on his haunches and offered Little Al some M&Ms. Rowanne helped Yazz to her feet: "Are you okay sweetheart?"

"Aye but ..." she panted, "we're, uh ... in a spot of bother." Yazz let out a blast of air, "Had a run-in with the guy we're staying with." Yazz stood upright and her thumbs slid under the lapels of the leather jacket. "I'm just borrowing this, so I am," she said looking up at Rowe with an innocent smile.

"Well, are you gonna get a room here?" Rowe asked.

"Here? Stay at a hotel? Ehm ..."

"My travel guide says it's reasonable, a family room with a full continental breakfast for thirty-eight guilders. You wanna share the cost of a room?" Rowe said, raising her eyebrows.

"Ehm, I don't know. I have nay looked in my

pockets. Let's see."

In Mal's inside jacket pocket, Yazz pulled out his wallet stuffed with a wedge of fifty-pound notes.

"Ehm, I got a bit spare. Let's do it."

"You're a lifesaver. I'm Rowanne, this is Darren."

"Hello, I'm Yazz and this is Little Al," Yazz replied.

"I'm running the marathon tomorrow," Rowe added, swishing her backpack to flash her trainers at Yazz, and again Darren bobbed out the way. "Och, aye – go you!"

*

Blair and Aitch ran to Cherry's Citroën and stopped dead, right in the middle of the road. The back passenger side door was open. Cherry was gone. Blair sank to his knees and picked up one of her ballet pumps from the tarmac.

Headlights lit up the two men and they both ran into the side of the abandoned car. "Where the hell is she?" Blair said, slamming her shoe on the roof.

"There's no blood on the road," Aitch replied.

Blair looked at the road where the shoe had been, then back to Aitch.

"Fu— Fuck it, get in, we gotta find Little Al

and Yazz," he said, tossing Cherry's pump on the back seat.

Blair's burned fingers fumbled to find the ignition key. "Bloody women!" he said as the car rose to life and he peeled away from the curb swiftly back into the nighttime traffic.

*

Mal held his hands out, the big man, alone in the darkness of the small cell, trying to focus. Mal's straight nose and chiselled features etched from the moonlight of the barred window. The chiaroscuro monster sat still, trying desperately to see straight, staring at his splayed, supine fingers. He began to rock, gently. The rich taste of Sambuca was gone and he withdrew into his mind where he imagined his life as a room, held up by a steel pillar. In this dark, imaginary space he saw a chalkboard; his life written on it; now a mess of lists, goals, quotes, sketches, tastes and feelings, all intertwined and overlapped. Through the dark liquorice, lust and mayhem there had been a maelstrom of confusion which had completely obliterated his chalkboard, now nothing made sense. As long as the boy and the crazy Glaswegian lass were okay, he hoped he could wipe the chalkboard clean and start again. He rocked and wept and without calling on God, prayed and promised for a new chapter in his life to begin.

*

Aitch was wired, he could feel the clock ticking. The lights were all on in the apartment as he and Blair examined every inch of it for some kind of clue. The adrenaline made Aitch giddy, his mind was racing, trying hard not to contemplate the dangers Yazz might be in, so he went to the bathroom to splash some water on his face.

Think straight. Blair studied the blood spatters on the fridge. Aitch reached for the cold tap at the bathroom sink, but stopped himself, noticing some blood on the side of the unit.

He looked closer at the small-ish, feminine fingerprints. They looked familiar, "Blair … come and look at this." Blair appeared and got down on his haunches to look closely. Aitch continued, "These are Yazz's fingerprints," he said. Blair gave him a so-so look.

Aitch pulled some paper from his pocket and showed Blair the outline of Yazz's hand that she had drawn on the last page of her letter. "See," Aitch said.

"Nice job, pen-pal boy," Blair said. "Let's keep looking."

Aitch nodded, feeling like they might be getting somewhere and walked into the bedroom. He emptied out Little Al's bag: a water bottle, some toys and crayons fell out on the bed. He picked up the large 1994 AA road map of Great Britain next to the bed and flicked through the pages. Just as Blair walked in, a slip of paper gently floated out like a feather. Aitch picked it up. A beaming smile came across his face.

Aitch passed the note to Blair.

"Uncle Mal, Yazz has taken me out on a secret adventure. AL"

Blair nodded and exhaled, extended his fist. Aitch bumped it with his and smiled.

"Okay, I'm going to search for them at the Leidseplein, I know the guys at Club Candela," Blair said. "You stay put in case Little Al and Yazz come back."

"You can't leave me! What if Eric or somebody else turns up?" Aitch replied. Blair signalled Aitch closer.

"I chucked two sleeping pills in Eric's gob, he's gonna be out for the count. Look, you gotta hold the fort, lad. Just keep the door locked and if anyone does come in …" Blair pulled back a curtain and opened the window to show Aitch "… just jump out on the fire escape. Got it?" And with that he walked out the door.

Aitch stood there for a few eternal seconds, lost in the white space. He turned a full three-sixty, breathed out deeply, went to the door, locked and bolted it. He turned back to the empty space and shook his head and shivered in his damp clothes.

"Bloody Judas! Breath … breath." Aitch looked up at the small Swiss railway-style clock on the wall: 2.47 a.m.

Damn! He needed a cocktail stick, something. Aitch paced around, feeling the cold and realised he needed to dry his clothes. He made a beeline for the kitchen and saw the washer/dryer and figured he may as well.

He slipped out of his clothes, stuck them in the machine for fifteen minutes and stood in his underwear. As soon as he heard the dryer door lock, he felt vulnerable. He opening the magnetic cupboards and slick drawers, searching the neatly stacked contents. On the sideboard, Aitch eyeballed a giant wooden knife block next to a jar of Nescafé. Aitch pulled a large cleaver out, reinserted it and pulled out a few small blades, *hmm*. He turned to open the final, small cupboard, in which he found some coffee mugs and a plastic box of cocktail sticks. "Bingo!" Aitch triumphed, punching the air. "Now," he said, "warm up and stay awake." He grabbed the kettle, filled it with water and flicked it on. Aitch couldn't stand still and continued to pace anxiously about, talking to himself.

"What the hell just happened?" he said, turning to lean on the mirrored wall. It gave a little and he sprung forwards and inch. "What the fuck?" His eyes opened wide and he span around. The mirror was a door. Aitch slid his fingers in the opening and drew the door back. Lights came on automatically, revealing a state-of-the-art video production suite. "Flamin' hell,"Aitch said, agog. He stepped forwards into the suite and turned, looking back out at the apartment from behind the mirrored glass. The kettle began to boil. "Flamin' hell," he said again, his mind racing.

He dashed out of the suite and switched off the kettle. He hopped from one foot to the other, spilling granules of Nescafé. He poured the boiling water into the mug and the granules dissolved with a satisfying plume of bitter froth, the rich aroma pushing his bladder over the edge. "Flamin' hell!" he said desperately, clutching his abdomen all the way to the toilet.

*

Yazz parted the boy's sweaty hair off his forehead to the left and withdrew carefully from the bed. Across the room Darren and Rowanne faced away, asleep, Rowanne's trainers together, next to the bed, her running kit laid out on a chair. Yazz rolled her eyes and lit a half-smoked joint by the window, looking out at the city.

*

Blair moved from one foot to the other, his hands stuffed in his pockets outside a club. Eventually a man in a suit joined the doormen, had a word with Blair, giving him a conciliatory nod that sent him on his way, gritting his teeth.

*

The dryer still had five minutes to go. Aitch rocked from one foot to the other, opening and closing the slick, kitchen drawers. He sipped the coffee, which was black and still way too hot. He set it down next to the sugar bowl and two small, sharp kitchen knives. They could be useful. Aitch slid the five-inch blade across his thumbnail. "Holy crap!" He stopped before it sank in too far, spelling 'S-H-A-R-P' in his head. *Careful, be ready*, he thought, preparing himself, then placed the knives down carefully. He added a cold splash of water to his coffee, then picked up the knives again and looked around the room, sussing out his options.

*

Yazz felt her head nod onto the cold, hostel window, turned and easily slipped off Mal's huge leather jacket, which fell to the floor with a muffled thump. Darren's eyes opened at the sound of Yazz's head on the window and watched her stumble onto the bed, kicking off her shoes, sliding in behind Little Al, her head falling on to the pillow, exhausted.

*

Aitch considered his options from behind the mirrored safety of the video suite, drinking the last of his coffee. Could he run with a knife? In front of him, the nine- and five-inch blades. He got up and ran from one side of the apartment to the fire escape trying to hold the nine-inch knife carefully. *No, no, no,* he thought, waggling his head and going back to the kitchen, replacing the nine-inch knife. He took the five-inch knife from the suite and placed it on the outside windowsill, very carefully. He went back to the video suite and, counted – three, two, one – and went for a final practise run from one side of the apartment to the other. He darted across the space, threw out his hand to grab the five-inch blade from the windowsill, mistimed it and tapped the knife over the edge. Aitch stuck his head out the window, saying, "Oh shit!" and a nanosecond prayer that nobody was below. He looked back to the front door, stuck to the spot, then looked again outside. "Fuck it!" he said, and ran to the front door, opened it and stopped himself, standing there in just his underwear. The dryer played a jingle and with that Aitch dressed himself in the freshly warmed clothes and bolted out the front door and down the stairwell. As he burst out the main entrance door, Morten, Cain and Ville stopped in their tracks before him, "Excuse me," Aitch exclaimed, his fingertips holding the door open for them a second, as he raced outside.

The lift door just closed as Aitch ran back in, before pegging it back up the stairs to the apartment. He shut the door and replaced the knife on the windowsill. He gasped, holding his chest, panting, bent over. Aitch's stomach growled and a tiny flutter fart came out, "Oh shit!" he said, and ran to the toilet. He let out a huge sigh of relief, his arse wedged in the seat, wishing this to be over, fast! He saw a switch with a fan icon and pressed it. The extractor came on. Aitch turned to his left and that seemed to move things along a bit, he turned to the right and with that, lost a good deal of himself in the toilet. Next to him, Mal's newspaper lay on the floor. The cover story about the Swedish bike gang war, featured an image of a biker, covered in his Badbones ink, looking directly at the camera, menacing and resolute.

Through the sound of the extractor, three clear knocks on the front door got Aitch sat bolt upright. His fingers crept up the wall and turned off the light and then to the other switch, killing the extractor.

Aitch tried to stand and stopped. He reeled some toilet paper like candyfloss on his hand, cleaned up and chucked it down the pan before returning his arse quickly to the warm seat. "Why me? Why now!" he said to himself quietly.

Somebody knocked again, this time a gentle rhythmic knock, almost friendly. Aitch poked his head out of the toilet door. Morten spoke, "Hey, so sorry to disturb you neighbour, I'm Timo, I just moved into the flat downstairs." Aitch buttoned up and walked silently and stealthily through the apartment.

"I just need to borrow some sugar. My brother has just arrived from Stockholm." Aitch listened intently and side-stepped a tote bag but caught his foot on the handle, knocking into the plates on the drainer. "Please?" the voice continued.

"Um, sure, sorry, I was in the bathroom and couldn't hear you." Aitch said, picking up the sugar bowl, side-stepping to the door which he slowly opened on the safety chain. On the other side of the door Ville held a gun to Cain's back, out of sight of Aitch. Morten leaned in to see more of the apartment.

"Wow, what a great space, it's way bigger than mine."

"Oh, this isn't my place, I've just ended up here," Aitch blurted.

"Oh, yeah?" Morten replied, offering a friendly hook.

"Longest day of my life," Aitch continued, feeling warmth in the discourse.

Morten took a step back, not rushing the kid.

"Why don't you join us for a coffee downstairs? My brother and his mate have just gotten in on the overnight train from Stockholm. He's an S.O.G. man, he'll fight the moon telling his war stories. And … I have some sweet Hulkberry grass if you really want to unwind." Morten said with an easy smile.

"I can't, I gotta stay put," Aitch snapped. "Wait." Aitch stopped himself. "S.O.G., that's Swedish special forces right?" as he remembered the countless hours spent as a child sketching military outfits from a library book on extended loan. Morten nodded. Aitch taking it all into the gills, holding the sugar bowl, carefully.

"Tell you what, why don't you all come up here in, say, five minutes for a coffee and a smoke?" Aitch countered with gleeful enthusiasm.

"Cool. That's very kind of you. See you in five …" Morten agreed with a pregnant pause.

They introduced themselves, Aitch smiled and Timo nodded as Aitch closed the door and put down the sugar bowl with a huge sigh of relief, bowing his head. "Thank you, Lord. The cavalry has finally arrived."

CHAPTER EIGHTEEN

The chair leg quivered as Eric swung his feet backwards underneath him. The seat kiltered forwards and he threw his body backwards, blinking as the chair passed the moment of no return. With a crack and an *oomph!* the chair smashed into the kitchen floor, deconstructing under his bodyweight. He wiped his face on a broken arm of the chair, removed the gag and took a panic breath. Stop, something was lodged in his throat. His eyes sprang open and he tried to clutch his neck, forgetting that he had a wok glued to one hand and the other lame arm was agony to lift. He gagged. Eric used all his might, fighting the pain to turn on the tap with his lame arm. *Stop*, he thought, if he swallowed the sleeping pills, Harry would make him disappear after Mal. The tap ran and kept running. He stared at it a second, wheezing, thinking, his eyes watering, he had one chance, time was running out.

*

The three Swedes stood outside the apartment in silence. Ville at the back, pressing his pistol roughly into Cain's side with explicit instructions directly in his ear: "Eric and Blair may be inside – ID them and you'll buy your freedom." Ville disengaged the safety with an ominous click, and reiterated, "Don't fuck with me." Swallowing hard, Cain replied softly "Okay ... brother," with a gentle smirk.

*

The salt cellar lid span off and Eric held the glass wok lid full of water precariously on the counter and chucked the entire contents in. He lifted his hand up with the bastard lid glued to it, swishing and slopping the cloudy liquid over the rim. In one shot he poured and slopped the violent saline solution over his meat encrusted white tombstones and into the dry cave of his mouth. It hit the mark like the thunder strike of a circus hammer. The spew shot up Eric's body with such fury it burned his windpipe and nostrils as it chundered out of his mouth and nose, ringing a bell in his head. His stomach pulsated and his body spasmed as the next vomit rocket-launched. Guinea fowl, potatoes, asparagus, wine, cheese, chocolate and the two sleeping pills splashed up the cupboards, sides, the sink and across the floor. Eric trembled and tried to grab the sideboard with his weak hand; it slipped and he fell to the floor with a scream, his wok hand out in front. The glass lid smashed as it hit the lino, the inertia of the fall sending Eric sliding across the floor openmouthed, dredging his own vomit. He lifted his head, spat and spat, puke up his face and in his eyelids, eyelashes and hair. Sitting up, he looked at what was his wok hand, now a jagged explosion of glass. He needed his fucking toffee hammer and a fucking glass of water, then, as soon as he could release his trigger finger, his fucking pistol.

*

The kettle was beginning to boil when the friendly knock came. *Pa, pa, pa, pa!* Aitch had never been happier to answer a door. The three bikers entered. Morten turned to the other two, "Wow, I told you this place was massive. Just you here, Aitch?"

"I'm Cain and this is my brother, Ville," Cain said, pointing to Ville who forced a smile.

"Yup! Hi, chaps – *sooo* glad you are here," Aitch said, now grinning as he turned to make the troops their coffees. "How do you take your coffee?"

"Just three black coffees, please," Ville replied.

"Three black coffees for three brothers." Aitch smiled at the trio, then turned to get down three mugs. Behind Aitch, Ville manoeuvred Cain onto the sofa. "Wait." Aitch turned to the amigos. "I thought one of you takes sugar?" Ville prompted Cain with his pistol.

"Guilty!" Cain said, throwing his left hand up in a small salute.

Ville and Cain sat on the couch, MTV playing in the background. As Morten rolled a joint, Cain took a good look at Aitch making the coffee. Ville tapped Cain with his pistol and raised his eyebrows. Cain screwed up his lips and gave Ville a 'maybe' bob of his head. "So, man, you said you just had the longest day of your life?" Morten asked, glimpsing up at Aitch as he set the coffees down and passed the sugared one to Cain. "Here you go, one with sugar." Cain nodded in thanks.

Morten passed Aitch the joint and a lighter. "I was supposed to be spending the weekend with a girlfriend in Liverpool," Aitch started, incredulously, as he tried to light the joint. Just sparks. Aitch felt about in his pocket, pulled out his own lighter, along with a few odd pennies. He lit the joint and took a lug, then leaned in conspiratorially. "We met this crew of Liverpudlian dealers and got split up and now she's here with one of them." Aitch looked at the trio on the sofa.

"Fucked up, right?"

"If she left with another guy, why did you bother to follow her out here?" Morten asked sitting forwards. The other two held their positions, but Aitch could feel something strange in the intensity of their eyes.

"She's wearing my jacket …" Aitch laughed nervously, and the looks in their eyes became perplexed.

"It has my wallet in it!" Aitch added.

Cain guffawed and Ville began to chuckle. Morten waggled his head in disbelief, resting the foot of his boot on the low table. "Who doesn't love their wallet?" Aitch smiled as he passed Morten the joint. Morten reached forwards and clear as day Aitch read Badbones tattooed on his wrist in Gothic lettering. As Morten took a lug, he asked "What are the names of these Liverpudlian dealers?" Aitch double-took the tattoo, felt adrenaline rush through him anew, and sat up dead straight with a cough. Morten leaned back and his boot pushed the table a little and the pennies dropped on the floor, spinning. Aitch set his foot on the pennies, dragged them over to him and took a sip of his scolding, black coffee. "Whoop, that is hot! Goes straight through me too," he said wiping his brow and setting down the coffee. "I gotta take a slash." Aitch tried to stand but the Huckleberry grass had turned his legs to jelly and he wobbled to the toilet.

Aitch locked himself in the toilet pulled out

the crumpled newspaper and flipped anxiously to the article on the Swedish biker war. He dropped his trousers and sat on the toilet, looking at the huge biker with his Badbones tattoo and insignia. He took a scared pee, quietly berating his situation. "Fuck, fuck, fuckety fuck-nuts. Hi, I'm Timo, I'm your neighbour ... bullshit. You want to lie to me, I'll give you a lie."

Aitch buttoned up and got on his hands and knees and opened the door quietly, slowly peeking around the corner nice and low in the darkness. "Hey," Morten said from up above. Aitch stopped, then looked up to his right, his forehead stopped by the cold barrel of Ville's pistol. Frozen in terror for an agonising second, Aitch raised his hands, his breathing staccato. Ville slowly lowered the Glock. Letting out the breath he'd been holding, Aitch collapsed on the tiled, toilet floor, sensing the gun above him.

Morten wedged himself into the cramped space, looming over Aitch intimidatingly. "Who exactly did you come to Amsterdam with?" Morten said. Aitch felt intensely cold and looked at the blank white tiles, mustering a partial truth through his adrenaline overdose. "Pie" he blurted, "a scouser who goes by Pie ... on account of his short, cropped hair, like a pie crust," Aitch blathered, his instincts overtaking any concerted breath.

Trying not to appear too interested, Morten

followed up, "This Pie, did he mention anyone called Eric?" Aitch was afraid to look up and face the gun, but knew this was a bartering tool. "We ... we stopped at Eric's earlier tonight."

"Good ... got the address?" Ville prompted.

"It's in my P— pocket," Aitch added.

"Give it to me," Morten demanded and Aitch reached down slowly to fish it out.

Morten plucked it out of Aitch's hand. That was it, his last card played. Aitch was scared rigid and he closed his eyes a moment, heard their clothes move, a soft click and footsteps. He thought he heard the door close. Aitch waited a moment. Nothing, so opened one eye. Still nothing. He scampered towards the door, doing a full three-sixty, looking around at the empty apartment. He bolted it and picked up the phone. He stood there, alone again, incomprehensibly shaken, unable to think or move, warm tears crawled out the corners of his eyes and dribbled down his face. Aitch took two deep lungfuls of air, trawled his sleeve across his face and ran his finger down the telephone directory, finding Club Candela. He noted the address and flicked to the front of the directory and found it on a map of the city. Aitch was getting out of here.

CHAPTER NINETEEN

Bloody droplets plinked rhythmically into the soapy dishwater from Eric's glass-encrusted hand. Turning on the sideboard lamp, he grimaced in pain, as he tried to make headway between teasing out the clear glass sceptres with a scalpel and picking razor shards off with tweezers. Since he'd turned the light on, the caterwauling outside was persistent. Eric continued to pick off the glass. Sasha would not stray from her routine. She was outside, but inside too. In his face, in his mind. He could feel the cat pushing into his arm. The joy of Sasha's purr, vibrating through him. Eric could move his fingers – 'Fuck it! He would get away from the smell of his own vomit, steal a minute of fresh air, feed Sasha, shower, change and go. He'd be hunting down Blair in fifteen minutes. Eric reached quickly into his drawer, removed a small Beretta pistol and grabbed a pouch of cat food before venturing out.

*

Eric scanned the shadows of the moonlit courtyard and called gently for Sasha. Her bell tinkled nearby and he got down, ready to dole out the food. The large, Norwegian forest cat wound herself eagerly around his glass encrusted hand, sniffing curiously. Eric basked in the rare moment of tenderness as the bushy-chested cat gave him a look, before chowing down on her terms.

*

The door was open. Morten turned to Ville to stay back with Cain. He entered, his feet splashing in the sick. He double-took the stinking mess. A few seconds later he reappeared to Ville and his captive, ushering them in. Ville nudged Cain to enter. "What the fuck!" Ville said quietly to his brother over Cain's shoulder as he closed the front door behind them. Morten began combing through the living room drawers and scanned photo albums. Several pictures showed Eric with a smiling blond man in gaudy rings and a penchant for tracksuits – a Run Zygo 93 banner in the background.

Morten turned to Cain. "Which one of these is Eric?"

He held the picture and continued snooping,

pressing PLAY on Eric's blinking answering machine. Cherry's concerned voice filled the tense silence, "I hope you are okay Eric, I heard what happened. Call me."

The machine peeped and the second message played, "Eric, you are my head of security, so when I call, you answer. Where the fuck are you when I need you? Send the Surinams back to Cherry's, the location has been … compromised. Call me back immediately!" Ville's eyes narrowed, meeting Morten's, "Play that last one again."

*

Sasha finished, licked Eric's hand once and left. The ritual was complete. Next he had to get the sick mopped up and shower – this was taking way too long, he'd have to step on it. Reaching the top of the stairs, Eric heard the answering machine and fast-paced it down the hallway to his apartment. His ears pricked … he heard movement and the door was now shut.

He pulled out his pistol and looked at his limp left hand. He replaced his gun in his trousers and put his door key in his left hand, his thumb and forefinger could just about manage the key. He slid it slowly into the lock, turned it and held it shut using the key, pulling back gently. He drew his pistol again, foot against the door to apply pressure. He counted down silently from three.

Morten turned back to Cain angrily. "Which one is Eric?" Ville pushed the pistol into Cain and the prisoner pointed to Eric as the door flew open. Morten eyes darted to the door. Ville and Cain turned to see Eric's pistol outstretched and Cain shoved Morten as the first round went off, clipping Morten's shoulder as he fell.

Eric charged forwards screaming, splashing through the vomit. Eric swung his Beretta left and fired over at Ville. He was ready, and let two rounds go as he trailed Eric who jumped to the floor behind the kitchenette. Cain saw Ville's outstretched arm and ducked under it and out the door. "Cain!" Ville barked, as Morten called out, clutching his right shoulder, "I'm hit!" Ville gritted his teeth at the scenario turning to shit and unleashed fury, shooting the pans hanging down from the kitchenette, *pang, ping, pong*. The heavy metal fell on top of Eric as Ville hauled his brother out the door. Eric popped his arm up on the kitchen counter and returned a shot, missing the back of Morten's head by a millimetre. Eric held steadfast a moment, eyes down the barrel, his arms parting the pool of his own cold puke.

CHAPTER TWENTY

Sunrise. Warm light angled down, filling the city, revealing the details of the medieval architecture and reflecting the tall skinny houses by the canal. The rays energised the domes of the runners as they tied laces, hydrated and stretched out in the open space known as Liedseplein. Rowanne looked out of the window watching other runners marching to the starting area as she gave her hamstrings a full extension, one leg up on the windowsill. Darren was stuffing yesterday's undies and a towel into his backpack. "I'm still tight, Darren. Have you seen my orb?" Darren looked at her: "You're what?" She glared back at him with her instruction. "See if my orb has rolled under the bed, please, my sweet prince." Darren smiled, and got down into a plank to snoop under their bed for her physio ball, his body an inch off the old carpet. Across the room he saw the ball and something else. He went over to the other bed. "Found it. Found this too!" he said holding Mal's wallet.

*

The public payphone looked out over the canal, next to a little café. Morten sat at a mirrored table, Ville getting his ear chewed on the telephone. "I know, I know, we're tailing Eric now, what about the other guy – Blair. What's he look like? Where can we find him?" Ville replied.

"Blair is an ally with connections to the central flower market, he may be able to help you," Per said with pained breath. "Looks like Jesus, has a military tattoo on his right forearm of a bull terrier. Know what a bull terrier looks like?"

*

Keys jingled and the kid's tiny feet tap-danced outside the apartment door. "I gotta go pee," Little Al screamed pushing on the front door, which flung open, sending him towards the bathroom like a rocket. Yazz slipped Mal's huge jacket onto the low table. One side seemed to hang off her, she felt the weight missing. She felt in the pockets and fell to her knees. "Shit, shit, shit!" she chided. Her eyes caught the contents of the table. The pennies, a half-finished joint and the lighter; that was Aitch's lighter. *Aitch was here!* she thought, turning to look around as Little Al called out.

"There's a poo in the toilet. A poo in the toilet. Poo, poo!"

"Okay, okay, I'm coming!" Yazz replied running to assist.

Little Al pointed, Yazz looked. "That is a big boy poo," the boy concluded.

"Big boys are dirty," Yazz replied.

*

Mal's watch read 8.39 a.m. He played it cool, walking out of the detention area, nodding at the desk sergeant. He got to the main door, across to freedom, and as the door boomed shut Mal took off, building up his pace quickly into a sprint. He ran down the Marnixstraat passed runners trooping in the other direction, voice raised, his arm up partly to shield his sore eyes from the sun, partly to clear the athletes from his path. The clock ticking.

*

Rowanne stopped her tally of deep squats and came over to Darren as he rifled through the wallet's contents, now scattered across the rumpled bedsheets. Pulling out a faded ID photo, Darren noticed something familiar. "Feck! I know this guy! Malcolm Tanner – Malcolm Tanner,

Rowe!" She looked at Darren blankly. "Legendary bodybuilder," he continued. Rowanne shook her head. "Cover model back in the 80s. Went by Mal 'the Body' Tanner," Darren continued. "Oh!" Rowanne said dryly. "He's the reason I got into bodybuilding, babe."

"Okay," Rowanne said as she came over and looked at the ID and picked up a scrap of paper from the wallet's contents, strewn across the bed. "This is an address in Amsterdam!" she said with an excited smile. "Let's pop it back after *my* run and *you* can meet your hero!" she said, thrusting the ID back at him.

*

Morten held the photos from Eric's apartment as he and Ville watched the main stage; the Run Zygo Marathon 1994 about to begin. Harry took to the stage. Ville held his hands up to focus his eyes better; Harry in a maroon tracksuit and headband at the mic. "Welcome, everyone. Just a notice that the kids' 5K race will begin shortly, raising valuable moneys for the ZyGo Children's Trust, so please do cheer us on and donate as much as you can to the ZyGo Volunteers. Let's hear it for the volunteers! See *you* at the start line!"

Morten tapped Ville. "Holy shit, that voice, that's the voice on Eric's answering machine."

"The boss. Harry Van Zyl is *the* boss!" Morten

nodded approvingly, the photo of Harry crumpled in his tightening fist.

*

Yazz marched around the apartment; staring at the white walls had begun to make her lose focus and she felt dizzy. Scooching between the couch and the low table, Yazz's right foot slipped on something and she fell straight on her skinny butt. The jolt made her wince in pain. Looking by her foot she reached forwards to pick up the curved white object – a tiny lighter. She brought it close to her face to examine it and recognised it immediately. "Aitch?" Yazz said and span the ignition wheel. She appraised the lighter and her bitten thumbnails for a moment. *Where was he?* she thought, and her heart began to race. Yazz ran into the bedroom fast as lightning. Little Al was laid on the bed with his personal stereo on. Yazz ran back out into the living area, ending up at square one, just panting and slightly deflated.

The front door opened. Yazz turned and her excited eyes met Mal's. The big man was beleaguered, panting and sweating. She stopped so quickly, she fell back, cowering, arms protecting her face, expecting another explosive tirade. But Mal's voice was gentle, even apologetic. "Thank God you're here," he said. "I'm ... I'm sorry." As she peered out cautiously from between her arms, he crouched down and wiped the tears from his eyes. "Last night," he exhaled, "was a big mistake. Please, forgive me, lass." Stunned by this sudden shift, Yazz could only stammer, "Really?"

Mal affirmed his regret, "Really. Last night … some mad shit happened here and after you left, made me think … different."

As relief washed over her, Yazz explained, "Yesterday you'd made me feel so comfortable and safe like … I imagine a dad would, and then … you know … I"m dead sorry for lamping ya!" Yazz held her breath. Mal looked away and then back to her.

"You're an honest-to-God firecracker," he replied and Yazz exhaled the last of her fear.

"You gonna be my friend then for another half an hour?" he said, looking up from his watch with a half-smile. Yazz managed a smile back. "Can you look after Little Al whilst I pop out and see a man about a dog? He is here, right?"

Yazz nodded and laughed.

"…and I'll be back here by 10.45."

Mal put on his jacket and pulled out a washbag from his wheeled case, which he put inside his coat pocket.

"Still warm. Thanks." Mal raised his eyebrows and ran to the door.

"Mal!" She called, stopping him, "we, um, we used some of your dosh to stay at a hostel last night. Sorry… and I …"

Mal turns and made a finger gun and grinned while he shot her. "No time. Don't worry about it lass!"

Yazz cracked a nervous smile, underlining her wet eyes.

Mal bolted out of the apartment door into the bright sunshine, the light was so bright it took him a moment. He looked at his watch, 9.54 a.m. A bike bell chimed as Mal hopped off the curb and the cyclist caught Mal's jacket, spinning him around and sending the skinny bearded rider palms-first into the tarmac. The skinny guy peeled his face off the gravel as Mal swung his leg over the bike and rode off.

The adrenaline paled and Mal's hamstrings became heavy. Shit! He hadn't done any cardio for years. The old muscles needed oxygen. The streets were busy, Mal was labouring, neck like a lubricated owl, navigating runners and trams, his thumb brushing the bell on repeat, sweat filling his eyebrows and trickling into his eyes. He doubled down, the market garden was close. He pedalled right up to the entrance, past rows of VW vans lined up outside the huge building and an HGV reversing into one of the many delivery bays. Mal braked minimally and dismounted in motion, the bike toppling behind him. Mal continued, striding forwards, flashing his buyer's badge at security as he made his way into the flower factory. Crossing the threshold, Mal felt the power and dynamism of the factory ever-present in the sound of automation: conveyor belts, carts, lifts and trolleys. He weaved around the giant, colourful automated carts which moved the vast quantities of flowers. Mal changed gear to a confident march, now in this familiar bubble and on time for the drop-off. This felt good, so much so, Mal cast his mind to this afternoon, he'd take his little family to the best spots on the beautiful canals, maybe visit the Wave bar.

*

A key tried to open the apartment. Yazz came over to the door, calling hopefully: "Aitch?" Nothing. She looked through the spyhole. Eric stood back to show himself, a bag of shopping nestled under his left arm, which was in a sling, his hair swept across his forehead. He pulled down his tinted glasses, looking over the soft brown lenses. "Hi, I am here to deliver the groceries and do some cleaning for the owner. Sorry, I didn't realise anyone was here. I can come back."

"That's okay, pal. You gonna be okay with yer arm like that?" said Yazz, opening the door.

"I'll be fine," Eric replied.

*

The sprinter van's peep was swallowed as it

reversed up to the din emanating from one of the factory's despatch bays. The back doors creaked open ready to receive the goods. A portly worker, in well-worn overalls, chewing gum, wheeled a six-foot trolley with a plastic liner out of the van and set it down. He spat the gum into the liner, smoothed his scruffy goatee and pushed both his gloved hands back by his ears. He wiggled his wet nose, ran his hands over his slicked-back receding hair, before finally drawing his right forefinger under his leaking facial tap. Looking up the worker saw Mal about forty feet away, and lifted his snotty glove to beckon him over.

*

Their shoes made no sound as Aitch and Blair ran down the avenues of flowers. From high above, the massive factory was like a super-slushie tongue of vivid colours and smells, its open bays blooming with daylight as bright and square as day-one dentures. Mal and the worker just tiny, dark silhouettes, seemingly insignificant morsels in the mouth of this voracious factory.

*

Eric unpacked the bag of shopping. Yazz and Little Al sat on the couch watching MTV. "Orangina?" Eric offered, holding out the textured glass bottle.

"Gawn then, it's nae Irn-Bru but I love those wee bottles," Yazz conceded and watched as the guy turned and grabbed two teaspoons from the drawer. He was making heavy weather of opening the two drinks, finally, reaching up to the cupboard of mugs to pick out a couple of straws. Orangina reminded Yazz of her first school trip to Paris; the excitement, the newness of everything French. Mal would be home soon and he seemed in a good mood, she had high hopes for this afternoon.

*

When Blair and Aitch turned the corner on the long loading bay, Mal was halfway to the worker, walking in and out of the sunlight blasting in from their left.

From the right, a man with short dark hair, in a dark blue loose chore coat appeared behind Mal pushing a cart of yellow roses. The man quickly pulled a pistol with a suppressor from his chest rig, holding it down in line with his body, pushing the cart with his other hand.

The worker motioned to Mal to stop in front of the six-foot trolley, opening his hand for the package. The worker stood to one side with a small blade, ready to check its contents. Mal sensed the flower cage behind him and turned as the chore coat opened and the hitman extended his arm, aiming a long pistol at him. Mal's eyes narrowed;

he'd dropped off here dozens of times, the initial danger he felt was gone, now in a split second it was back. Mal dove on the floor and rolled to hide down in the drop between the back of the van and the bay entrance. As the pistol fired, the hitman fell forwards, Blair, midair, one hand under the hitman's outstretched arm, the other, palm striking down the back of the guy's neck.

The shot clipped the worker, sending blood over some white tulips, and he dropped the package. Mal jumped up onto the bay as the worker staggered back clasping his shoulder. Mal grabbed the top pocket of the guy's workwear and fired his right hand like his target was behind the worker's head, sending snot, blood and teeth flying out as the worker fell backwards into the trolley.

Aitch stood rigidly by the cage of yellow roses. Blair stood up with the hitman, immediately pulling the guy's jacket down from the shoulders, the chore coat arms strapped to his sides. The guy's eyes were beady and close together on his shocked, pale face. Blair had him, and launched an uppercut to the diaphragm, bending the guy in half, wheezing. Blair sidestepped the guy, who was choking for breath, grabbed the collar of his coat and the guy's belt and pushed him off balance, forwards. Blair followed, his body weight dropping, his knee on the back of the hitman's neck, smashing the guy's face into the concrete.

Mal shouted, "Let's go!" and dashed towards

the sprinter van. He turned back at the driver's door expecting to usher Blair and Aitch in – all Mal saw was the machete. The worker was running at him screaming, swiping wildly at Mal with the hacking blade. The big man ducked and stepped sideways, falling awkwardly over a bucket of roses.

Blair was pummelling the hitman on the floor, so Aitch took a deep breath and ran to help Mal, the sound of his broken maraca appearing as he got towards the light.

Blair got to his feet shaking his bloodied, bandaged hand and immediately the hitman span over, tripping Blair. The hitman scrabbled for his gun, six feet away, and Blair grabbed the guy's legs.

Mal swiped a handful of roses across the worker's face, its thorns tore across the fat man's cheek, exploding red petals over the van. Mal jumped in the passenger seat, and seeing the assailant charging at him, opened the van door at the last moment. The podgy-faced, pony-tailed assassin chopped downwards with the machete wedging in the open doorframe. The worker tried to pull back on the machete as Mal slammed the door shut. The worker was off balance and Aitch ran into him like a train, sending the guy's bloodied, podgy face smashing through the closed passenger door window.

Aitch pinballed back, turning to see the hitman kick Blair in the face, dropping him. The hitman came in again and Blair grabbed the guy's foot, twisting his lower leg and pulling him to the floor. For a moment Aitch thought Blair was taking control, and he looked down to see the hitman's pistol. He thought about grabbing it and as he looked up to take action, to see the hitman had scrabbled up and was running at Aitch. The smart boy had no options, he just kicked the pistol under the hitman's feet back to Blair. The hitman grabbed Aitch by the throat, pushing him over the metal railings. The man's pale face and beady lifeless eyes drilling Aitch amidst the tension of their tangled arms. Aitch couldn't move the guy's hands, choking him out. He couldn't reach anything – if he punched the guy or took his feet off the ground he'd topple backwards over the rail. Desperately he pulled out the cocktail stick box from his pocket, as his feet edged backwards an inch and he felt a primal instinct. Aitch flipped off the cap and stabbed the wooden spikes into the hitman's cheek with a venomous strike.

The hitman, let out a wail, let go of Aitch and turned around on the railing. Blair was ready, on one knee, aiming down the barrel. The hitman's eyes furious at this turn of fate. *Pap, pap* and the hitman's knees exploded, flesh and blood flicked up on Aitch's face. His visceral reaction was instantaneous. His internal clutch popped and he spewed as the hitman bounced delicately in what seemed like slow motion off of the metal railing. The hitman keeled over slowly, his mouth was still open, Aitch's explosion of cocktail sticks still stuck in his cheek. The indelible moment was captured in Aitch's mind as the man's wiry, torn-up body fell into his fresh pool of vomit.

Blair grabbed Aitch by the arm and pulled him forwards, shoving the beleaguered lad into the long front seat of the sprinter van. "Thank you," Mal said, picking up the unopened package and jumping in the sprinter as it pulled away.

Tension crackled inside the speeding van as Aitch sat wedged between Mal and Blair. "Where the hell are Little Al and Yazz?" Blair erupted, his knuckles white on the steering wheel.

"Woah, woah, woah," Mal said, holding up his hands. "Somebody just tried to frikkin' top me, mate." Mal turned to Blair. "They're fine, Blair, they're at Harry's apartment – only left 'em there half an hour ago."

"The same people who tried to top you have some nasty shit planned for them, that's what … because of you, they're in real fucking danger," Blair spat, stepping on the accelerator.

The life drained out of Mal and was instantly replaced with anger in his eyes, his breathing built up to a raging fury as he punched the dash. "Aitch, use my mobile to call Yazz at the apartment. Speed dial five." Mal sat forwards and handed Aitch the phone.

Blair leaned forwards to look at Mal for a moment. "What's the fucking crack bringing Little Al here?"

"I couldn't let Paul take Little Al away on his first holiday," Mal said matter-of-factly.

Mal sat back. Aitch looked up from the phone, shaking.

"Th— this is not a holiday!" Aitch effused. Mal leaned forwards around Aitch.

"Just make the call, smart boy," Mal said. "What's the latest with the big man?" Mal continued, looking back to Blair.

Aitch brought the mobile to his ear, waving Mal off. "It's ringing, it's ringing!"

"He's in intensive care," Blair replied.

"He'll pull through, then we'll go hunting," Mal said, raising his eyebrows.

Blair turned to Aitch. "No answer," he said with a blank face.

Mal held out his hand. Aitch put the phone back in it.

"Right, hold this," Blair said to Aitch, passing him the hitman's pistol. Aitch held the alien item by the barrel. Blair turned to Aitch: "Fuck's sake, hold the grip. Safety is on. Here – see, ON, OFF. ON." Aitch felt conflicted even holding it. He turned it over in his hand, feeling empowered. He'd seen so much violence and danger in the last twenty-four hours, maybe this was the only way to save Yazz and Little Al. He had a moment of realisation, saw himself in the van, fully self-conscious about what he'd gotten himself into … serious shit! Suddenly,

ADAM LORETZ

Aitch was terrified.

CHAPTER TWENTY-ONE

An ominous quiet permeated Harry's studio apartment. Oblivious, Little Al lay with eyes closed, candy-hued headphones still thumping 90s beats. Nearby, Yazz's eyes blinked rapidly against an artificial fog clouding her thoughts, which slipped in and out of reality, *I'm so fucked! Mal's gonna kill us if I don't get his wallet back.* "Maybe I could drive to the hotel?" Yazz said, voicing her thoughts.

"What did you say?" Eric cut back.

Yazz squinted at the half-empty bottle, "This is nae Orangina!"

Eric raised his eyebrows above his glasses. "You're probably just tired."

"Naw, naw, what did you put in this?" Yazz snarled poking the bottle at him.

"Nothing," Eric replied. Yazz went straight to Little Al and shook him, he was lifeless.

Yazz turned and Eric was stood right by her.

"Fuck off!" she snapped and threw the orange in his face. Streaks of blue appeared as foundation ran down his cheeks, he batted the soaked glasses off and rubbed his eyes. Yazz pulled a tiny wrap from her bum bag and snorted it, grabbed Mal's car keys and launched herself towards the door, tripping over awkwardly, spinning around on her arse. Eric sprang between her and the exit "Whoa, you're not going anywhere!" he said, and grabbed her shoulder.

Yazz turned and punched him in the giant bruise on his face and lurched out the apartment.

Somehow Yazz made it to Mal's BMW, got it started and put her foot on the accelerator, sending it straight into the car behind. Shaken up, Yazz looked at the auto shifter, trying to focus. Eric slammed into the driver's door, hitting the window, his maniacal eyes drilling her. Yazz's bitten forefinger pressed the door lock a second before he tugged at the door handle. Yazz panic-pressed the Unlock All door button and Eric flew back as the door pinged open. Yazz engaged Drive on the shifter, swerved out wide, clipping the BMW's wing mirror on the cars parked on the opposite side of the street. She stopped to shut the driver's door and Eric appeared again, sticking his arm in to grab her. Yazz stomped the accelerator and the car fishtailed away, the door slamming on Eric's arm, pulling him onto the concrete as Yazz sped off. Escape was the only thought pounding through her addled mind as buildings streaked by in a nauseating blur.

*

The crowds applauded the runners as they crossed the finish line. The clink of coins being thrown into buckets added percussion to the cheers and clapping of the excited herd, packed tight along the metal barriers. Runners and their stencilled, long shadows crossed the finish line. Both kinds of marathon runner crossed the line: some had mastered the performance and others struggled, some finishing at a light jog, warming down, others in their shadow, agonisingly limping, their faces etched with desperation and exhaustion. Amidst the runners' agony and ecstasy, the volunteers actively collected donations. The runners with all different kinds of tears celebrated as the efficient street cleaners began to sweep away the morning's debris.

Her finishing medal felt heavy and cool as Rowanne rubbed it gingerly across her sweaty forehead before giving it a tiny kiss. She held Darren's hand as he eagerly led her, navigating with a map, through unfamiliar streets. Rowanne let go and trailed behind, walking stiffly, the half-marathon clearly having taken its toll on her. "Come on, slow coach!" Darren joked. Rowanne shot back "Look, I just ran thirteen miles and now

I gotta pee." Stopping to let her catch up, Darren threw open his arms theatrically. "I'm proud of you. You are awesome!" he exclaimed, enveloping his partner in an effusive hug. "Too tight!" Rowanne winced.

*

His heart was still thumping, a warm towel around his neck. "How long?" Harry called. Eric stood with a pinny on cooking a fry-up. "One minute," he said, pouring oil in a pan and getting the eggs out. Harry moved back into the edit suite, inserted a Mini DV cassette in to the main video camera. His forefinger closed the articulated door, tiny cogs and motors feeding the tape over the capstans. He let his finger stroke down the video camera to the red Record button. He checked his watch and moved to the edit-suite door, "I can't wait. Bring in the boy, let's revive him on the couch with the smelling salts." Harry went back to the camera and pressed Record.

*

Mal parked the sprinter van out of sight of the apartment and Blair dashed after him as Mal marched to the main entrance. Blair caught his arm and whispered in his ear. Aitch's guts felt ropey and he climbed out of the van carefully, following the two gangsters to the metal fire escape, Blair watching him. Aitch looked at the metal stairs and mouthed to Blair, "What the fuck?" Blair turned to him, his finger on his lips … "Strategy," he mouthed.

Harry put down the smelling salts and went to answer the soft knock at the door, his Luger in the small of his back, tucked in his waistband. The well-set Irishman broke a smile as the door opened, then his face dropped a little. "Oh, hi, I'm looking for Malcolm Tanner."

Harry replied, "I'm sorry, you must be mistaken, there's nobody here by that name," and shut the door.

Darren turned slowly, perplexed, around to Rowanne, sitting cross-legged by the top of the stairs. "That was a bit weird, Rowe. I had a feeling this would be the place."

"Me too," she said, her voice quivering, trying to stand with legs like jelly. "I really am bursting," Rowe continued as she breathed out slowly, letting her body slide over to him as she used the wall to take her weight.

They congressed on the small metal balcony which served the fire escape, Aitch passed Mal the knife on the windowsill and Blair the hitman's pistol. The young guy himself, trembling like a junior jackhammer. Blair turned to Aitch: "Breathe; you just check the bedrooms."

Mal turned to Blair, "Get ready: three, two …"

There was another soft knock at the door. Harry opened it on the chain, one hand behind his back ready to draw the Luger.

"… one", Mal popped the knife in his mouth and jumped up and in through the window. Knife in hand, he charged at Harry. Harry turned a millisecond before impact, knocking the knife from Mal's grasp. Blair rushed to flank Mal as Eric turned from the stove, launching the sizzling frying pan at him. The red-hot skillet boomed as it hit Blair's crossed arms, burning fat splashing Blair's face, the impact dropping him on his back.

Aitch had followed his orders and ran into the bedroom. Little Al lay still on the bed. Aitch felt the kids breath on the back of his hand.

The apartment door was still on the latch, the violence erupting in front of Darren's eyes. "Let's get out of here!" Rowanne pleaded, pulling Darren's arm. "Wait, there's our guy, there he is, there's Malcolm," Darren said as Harry span Mal around, drawing his Luger at him. Harry fired as Mal lurched forwards, grabbing Harry's wrist. The Luger flew out of Harry's hand as the two warriors span around, Mal crashing into the wall of mirrors and on the floor. That pushed Darren's button. The rugby player drew up his huge leg and kicked through the door, smashing it off the chain. "No!"

Darren shouted as he ran to stop Harry, who was now brandishing Mal's kitchen knife. Harry turned to Darren and Mal jumped straight up, headfirst into Harry's stomach, lifting him up and spinning him on his head. Darren tried to grab Harry's arms as he wildly slashed the blade back and forth. The razor-sharp blade lacerated the Irishman's palms and flicked blood across Mal. Harry was still being held tight, and he turned the knife over and stabbed down into Mal's shoulder. Mal stopped at the vicious puncture and fell forwards, dropping Harry on the low coffee table, destroying it as they hit the floor.

Darren ran into Rowe just inside the apartment door. She grabbed his wrists, to stop him running into her and stepped back, body-checking the front door. It closed behind her as Darren's bloodied hands left tribal marks on her face. Rowanne gave an ear-piercing scream, her eyes bulged and she immediately pee'd herself.

The scream went through Aitch and he ran out of the bedroom, his eyes instantly connecting with Rowe and Darren's. She was hyperventilating, the steam off her piss rose up, her face like stone, eyes locked amidst the incomprehensible extreme violence in front of them. Aitch waved them quickly to the bedroom. Darren picked her up and ran them into the bedroom. He sat her on the bed and covered her legs with the quilt from one of the single beds. Aitch grabbed a pillow.

"Look Rowe, it's Little Al" Darren said, pointing to the other single bed. Seeing Little Al gradually, calmed her down, "He's out of it, but he's breathing" Aitch said, "I checked," as he passed Darren a pillow case for his wounds, "here!"

Mal staggered about helplessly with the knife in his shoulder, unable to get a grip of it, spiralling out of control. Eric didn't take his eyes off of Blair as he pulled the bow of the pinny to release the Beretta which he had stuck in his waistband. He pulled the gun ready to make good on his promise to Blair, who was clambering to his feet. The gun went off and smashed a window pane as Mal stumbled forwards into Eric. Blair threw himself back on the floor, his head skidding into the fridge, into the line of sight of Aitch. This time, the unspoken connection triggered Aitch, who ran into the room, straight into Eric. They fumbled, Aitch grabbed Eric's pistol hand and the weapon fell as they struggled together across the room. Eric span his hand over Aitch's to gain control, shooting his arm up to grab Aitch by the neck, the small shards of remaining glass tore at Aitch's throat. Toppling quickly, Aitch could see the open window upside down and put his hands out to stop himself getting ejected from the third-floor window. He slammed into the open window and struggled, arms tight to his side as Eric tried to bring the window down on Aitch. The window slammed down hard as Aitch got an arm up, his elbow stopping the deadly motion. Aitch kneed

Eric's legs, freed his other arm, and drew up the lemon juice bottle from his trouser pocket, squirting it directly in Eric's eyes before pushing him away.

Aitch lifted his head from the windowsill to see Mal fall to his butt against the mirrored wall, taking short breaths.

The apartment door was kicked open and Ville and Morten stepped in, guns drawn. Morten turned his pistol to the left as Aitch moved in his peripheral vision.

Blair shouted, "Gun!" and pulled the fridge door open, shielding Aitch from Morten's bullet. Aitch looked down from the open fridge door and saw the hitman's gun.

Morten turned to the right as Eric picked up his pistol, Morten reacted, shooting him in the shoulder. Eric sank to his knees and Morten shot again. Aitch watched as blood exploded from Eric's head. Aitch stepped back slowly towards the mirrors, the other side of the kitchenette, out of sight of the bikers. Harry stood back by the kitchen cupboard with nowhere to go. Ville calmly shot Harry in the leg. Aitch stopped walking backwards, now inside the video editing suite, watching in third-person.

Mal fell forwards, the knife still in his back. Harry scrabbled up, clutching his thigh, still trying desperately to get away from Ville. "Do you know who I am? What I can do for you," he panted.

"You betrayed Badbones and put yourself in the middle of a war ... expect the crossfire," Ville replied.

"I ..." Harry tried.

Behind Ville, Morten stepped out holding a huge cleaver.

In the edit suite, Aitch stood aiming the hitman's gun at Morten through the glass. Morten stopped and handed the cleaver to Ville. "Here, I would do it, but ..." Morten grimaced at the bullet wound to his right shoulder.

Ville took the cleaver and a deep breath. He approached Harry with the cleaver up high, ready to execute the final blow. A bead of sweat ran down Aitch's brow. A shot rang out and the cleaver leapt from Ville's hands. All eyes turned to the doorway, Jada stood there with Harry's smoking Luger. Her dark glasses slid down the perspiration on her nose.

"Get away from my boss! Drop your gun!" she shouted.

Ville looked at the tracker on the girl's leg, "You must be ... the video girl. This man has made you a sex slave. Why would you want him to live?"

Jada admitted, "He was going to pay me today ... to make a film."

"Filming's cancelled," Ville said coldly.

Ville's hand relaxed in readiness to quick draw. Jada turned the Luger at Ville, moving into the room. "You wanna be first?"

Jada pointed to Morten, "You?"

Jada aimed at Blair. Momentarily relaxing her grip on the gun, at his familiar eyes, "Not you."

Jada tensed back up, pointing the gun at Ville.

"How much was he going to pay you?" Morten said, nodding towards Harry.

"$500 guilder," Jada said.

A soft voice came from the doorway, out of Aitch's sight.

"Um, hey, there's a wallet on the floor right behind you with over £1,000 in it." Jada waved Yazz in holding the Luger on Ville, and walked sideways through the puddle of Rowanne's urine. Yazz took the money from the wallet and handed it to Jada, who stuck it in her small cross-body.

Aitch aimed at Jada.

Jada stood with her gun still on Ville and then slowly walked up to Harry. Behind Jada, Yazz scampered across into the bedroom. Harry beamed at his rescuer, "Thank you, Jada, my angel," he said, letting out the tension, his eyes opening.

She turned to him, swiftly firing twice into his chest. "Fuck you."

Morten grimaced in angry disappointment.

Stomping his dying body she sliced off her

tracking bracelet and tossed it onto his bloody chest. She kept her eyes on Ville and Morten and slowly walked out backwards, just as she had walked in. She got to the door, lowered her gun, still staring at Ville and Morten, taking her moment of emancipation before disappearing.

Ville looked dumbfounded. He got out his pistol and gently pushed Blair's face to the floor.

Aitch covered his eyes. "Let me do this," Morten said and picked up the damaged cleaver in his left hand.

Blair looked at the floor as Morten hacked down with a thud and a crunch across the dead man's neck.

A plastic bag rustled and a zip ran its course. "What do we do about these two?" Morten asked coldly. Noticing Blair's tattooed arm, Ville asked, "Are you Blair?" Aitch's finger tensed on the trigger as Blair nodded. "Per says thank you," Ville replied, waving his gun to the door. Morten threw the gruesome bagged trophy over his shoulder and they left.

Aitch lowered his weapon with relief and walked straight to Yazz, her eyes wet with tears. Blair groaned on the floor trying to get up. Yazz embraced Aitch tightly amidst the carnage when a single shot rang out. They turned to see Eric standing there, gun pointing at them, his left ear hanging off, blood all over his face and neck.

He pulled the trigger again and again to

no avail. Empty, he dropped the gun and pulled the knife out of Mal's shoulder and ran at them screaming. Aitch swung Yazz aside and fumbled with the pistol, raising it up. Aitch pulled the trigger, but the safety was on. Eric drew the knife slightly higher, now toe-to-toe with Aitch. Yazz yanked Aitch and they fell down into the doorway entrance as Blair charged into Eric's back, grabbing his sides from behind and pushed the screaming, bloody man through the open window. Blair's body hit the window frame with a thud, knocking the air out of him, forcing him to watch Eric fall head first in to the pavement.

On the floor, Aitch slowly pulled back from Yazz, their noses touching, relief in each other's eyes. Blair emerged with Little Al in his arms, still out of it, but Blair could feel his little heart beating. The midday sun bleached out Blair's face, masking his emotions. Looking out the window, he spotted the bikers outside taking cover, he moved and kicked something, it was the hitman's pistol by his feet in the stinking urine. For once, this wasn't Blair's fight, he watched it unfold. A loudhailer squealed: "Drop your weapons and put your hands above your head."

The hardened bikers refused, exchanging fire with newly arrived police.

Morten threw a couple of smoke grenades and pulled a long clip from his duffle bag, unleashing twenty rounds, rapidly creating maximum chaos. The smoke blew gently across Morten's position. Blair moved in close to the window and waited for the scene to clear. Like that, the bikers were gone. Blair took in a new breath, held Al close and turned to Darren and Rowe who were wrapping ripped bedsheets around Mal's wound.

Yazz wriggled. "Get off, Aitch, I got something sticking in me?"

"Sorry" he said, sitting up.

Yazz pulled his wallet from his jacket, that she had put back on.

"Naw, I'm sorry."

"Doesn't matter, as long as you're okay," Aitch said, raising his eyebrows. She held him close and then held him at arm's length, "Next time, I can visit you in London …"

Blair turned to Rowe and Darren, pointing at Mal. "Let's get him to my van, please," he said, then turned to Aitch and Yazz, "we got to go pick someone up."

*

Nine days later. The VHS machine swallowed the cassette. White noise broke into a CCTV image, distorting, then clear. Frank's garage, cam two from the office, 3.38 a.m.

Pie ransacked Frank's office filing cabinet,

fruitlessly searching for something ... He stopped, and listened, then turned with a hammer. The video paused.

Printed in Great Britain
by Amazon